ALSO BY AMY REED

BEAUTIFUL

CLEAN

CRAZY

AMY REED

SIMON PULSE

NEW YORK LONDON TORONTO SYDNEY NEW DELHI

᛭

SIMON PULSE

An imprint of Simon & Schuster Children's Publishing Division
1230 Avenue of the Americas, New York, NY 10020
First Simon Pulse hardcover edition June 2013
Copyright © 2013 by Amy Reed
All rights reserved, including the right of reproduction
in whole or in part in any form.
SIMON PULSE and colophon are registered trademarks
of Simon & Schuster, Inc.
For information about special discounts for bulk purchases,
please contact Simon & Schuster Special Sales at 1-866-506-1949
or business@simonandschuster.com.
The Simon & Schuster Speakers Bureau can bring authors to your live event.
For more information or to book an event contact
the Simon & Schuster Speakers Bureau at 1-866-248-3049
or visit our website at www.simonspeakers.com.
Designed by Mike Rosamilia
The text of this book was set in Adobe Garamond Pro.
Manufactured in the United States of America
2 4 6 8 10 9 7 5 3 1
Library of Congress Cataloging-in-Publication Data
Reed, Amy Lynn.
Over you / Amy Reed. — First Simon Pulse hardcover edition.
p. cm.
Summary: A novel about two girls on the run from their problems,
their pasts, and themselves. Max and Sadie are escaping to Nebraska,
but they'll soon learn they can't escape the truth.
ISBN 978-1-4424-5696-9 (alk. paper)
[1. Friendship—Fiction. 2. Family problems—Fiction. 3. Mothers and daughters—Fiction.
4. Communal living—Fiction. 5. Farm life—Nebraska—Fiction. 6. Nebraska—Fiction.]
I. Title.
PZ7.R2462Ov 2013
[Fic]—dc23
2012023492
ISBN 978-1-4424-5698-3 (eBook)

For all my best friends—
past, present, and future

κάλλιστη

kallistéi

"to the fairest"

—*The Iliad,* Homer

Part I

Chaos came first.

Before you and me and everything that has been and everything that will be. Before the gods or even the idea of the gods. Just the promise of matter, just disorganized potential.

Every story starts with the Big Bang:

Once upon a time.

Sadie, this story is yours.

I am the storyteller and you are the story.

When you want to remember something, you always say "Tell me about that one time we—" then I fill in the blank, and I recount your memory.

I am the history keeper of us.

We've been sitting on our bags in the middle of nowhere for almost an hour.

"No one's coming," you say, always the pessimist. You sigh and pull at a sweaty clump of hair that's stuck between your temple and the giant sunglasses you always wear, the ones that cover nearly half your face and make you look like a movie star. "I thought Nebraska was supposed to be cold." Where you got that idea, I don't know. You have a lot of ideas. Maybe you're just confused—it must be hard keeping track when every time you see your mom she lives in a different place. It must be like getting stuck in some weird kind of feedback loop where you're being shuttled around millions of light-years through wormholes, lost in time and space, and every time you land it's somewhere and sometime new, and you have to get your bearings quick, even though you're dizzy and disoriented and nauseous and probably a little bit scared. Now we've landed on this planet where it's June and humid and a million degrees, and the wormhole looks more like a bus that dropped us off on the side of a dirt road in the middle of a never-ending expanse of fields, not even at a bus stop, just a spot that looks exactly like every other spot for miles and miles and miles.

We don't have cell reception, and I'm starting to wonder if your mom even knows we're coming to stay with her for the summer. Maybe we went back in time, to before my dad supposedly talked to her on the phone, before your dad got so desperate to get rid of you, before anyone made any arrangements. Or maybe she just forgot.

You look so small against the sky, even with your shit-kicking boots and pink hair and fluorescent sundress-of-the-day, all of these things that usually make you seem so much bigger than everyone around you. But now it's just you against the sky, and even you can't beat that. The sky's big here in a way it never gets in Seattle, where we're always so snug with all the mountains crowding from every direction. There are some sad hills in the distance here, but they seem like a backdrop, like something two-dimensional and only half real. The rest is dusty flat infinity and big blue sky that goes up and up and up. This is the kind of sky little kids draw. And it sounds like the inside of my head when I'm wearing earplugs. Everything is so still, except for the creepy shivering of the corn, like the part in a horror movie before everything gets crazy. Corn everywhere. Corn for miles. So many places for things to hide.

Something about this reminds me of an old Greek myth. I don't tell you this because I know you'd just roll your eyes and say *Everything reminds you of an old Greek myth*, which is probably a little bit true. But it really does feel like we're at the beginning of an epic journey—lost in the desert, exposed to the gods and the elements, trudging through the punishing heat toward vague promises of paradise. This is the beginning of our *Odyssey*, our search. But which of us is the hero? There can only ever be one.

But you're not concerned with that. At the airport, you announced that we'd be traveling as young socialites. You lifted your chin to the air and shifted onto one hip, put two fingers to your lips and smoked an invisible cigarette. You strutted through the Sea-Tac terminal as if it were your runway. I followed, the socialite's assistant. It felt like an important job. But now we're here, with no one but me to see you. I know you're depressed, but you still look beautiful.

I could just close my eyes and listen to the almost-silence.

But I know you're not so easily charmed. You're the one we have to worry about. And I am, as usual. Worrying.

What were you expecting, Sadie? How many ways are there to interpret your mom telling you she lives on a farm?

"Don't you know where the farm is?" I ask.

"How would I know where the farm is?"

"No one gave you directions?"

"My mom said Doff would pick us up at the bus stop."

I want to say *How does anyone even know this is a bus stop?* but I don't.

You start pacing back and forth, holding your cell phone in front of you like a divining rod.

"Dammit."

"Still no bars?"

You lift the phone above your head, spin around, hold it out in front of you, crouch, and hold the phone near the ground, as if one of these many configurations could trick the cell towers into thinking we're not in the middle of nowhere.

"Dammit!" You throw the phone at a row of corn.

"We should hitchhike," I say.

"In what car?"

Good point. We haven't seen a car in the hour we've been sitting here. You jump across a wide, dry ditch to retrieve your phone. You're on your hands and knees, sifting through the dust and dry grass. I don't have the heart to tell you you're now wearing a spiderweb as a hairnet.

You sit up with the phone in your hand, your tangled pink bob covered by its ghostly new accessory. You sigh, take one last heartbroken look at your phone, then leap back across the ditch and shove the cell into your backpack, your eyes slanted in fury as if betrayed.

"Let's walk," you say.

"But we don't know where to go."

"If we walk, we'll end up somewhere."

You assume I will follow. And I do.

You've been talking about your mom since we were little. I've seen pictures of her at the Great Wall of China, scuba diving in Belize, riding elephants in Thailand, and I have listened to your fairytale stories. Her greatest magic is the fact that she's not your father. Remember that time I asked you why you didn't live with her? You closed up tight, became a brick wall, turned to stone. You mumbled something about money, it was because of money, everything is always about money. It is the thing your mom doesn't have, the thing your dad has too much of. I didn't ask how you became their currency. I didn't ask how he came to own you. I didn't ask how she could afford to go to all the places in the pictures but not house a daughter more than a couple weeks per year. I didn't ask why she makes herself so hard to find, why she never stays more than a couple of years in one place, why she often forgets to give you her new phone number. This summer will be the longest you have been with your mother since you were a baby, since the brief few years your parents were still married.

You're tired and sweaty, and even you can't make this glamorous. I'm pretty sure you've given up on pretending we're socialites. That lost its fun shortly after our layover in Denver, but now you're making a decent go with this displaced-city-girl act. It's always something, even when the only audience is me and corn and some crickets. There's always a game of pretend to play; there's always someone else you want to be. Once I kidded you about how you should go into acting, and you lectured me about how all actors are "narcissists" and "egomaniacs with inferiority complexes" and how acting is the "most banal of the arts." I don't know how you insert words like "banal" into your vocabulary and make them sound like they belong there, or how you manage to cultivate all these opinions that you assert so passionately. All I know is you make a lot of proclamations, and whether or not you actually believe them, I usually do.

One of your favorite proclamations is that your dad is a douchebag. Supposedly, he didn't used to be a douchebag, of which you are the proof. At one time, long, long ago, he was someone your mother could love. We don't quite believe this, even though he will occasionally roll his eyes at one of your colorful outfits or pseudo-revolutionary statements and say something cryptic like *If you only knew me when I first met your mom*, like you're too late, you missed your chance to have a parent who actually understands you, and now you're stuck with this prematurely balding man who works seventy hours a week at a bank and drives a gas-guzzling four-wheel-drive Suburban, even though he never hauls anything around except his new brat kid and way-too-young and obnoxiously boring trophy wife and the occasional large electronics purchase. Sometimes we pass him in the kitchen on our way out the door, and these things just pop out of your mouth, things like *Dad, you're such a cliché*, and he does his *har har har* chuckle, and trophy wife Trish has no idea what anyone's talking about and just giggles like a drunk foreign exchange student.

And now we're here. A man can only *har har har* for so long. Someone was probably going to get murdered if you stayed in that house one more minute, and everyone worried it would be your four-year-old half brother, Eli, and I guess no one could think of anything better to do than to ship you off to the middle of the country. With me, of course. Everyone knows I come along with the package. Your dad's always saying how he holds me responsible for making sure that you're not dead or haven't been sold into white slavery.

"I'm tired," you announce. We've been walking ten minutes. You'd be a terrible slave.

Which does not bode well for our summer plans. Because even though I know you've been fantasizing about a different kind of mother from the one you've always known, we both know we're not here for quality family time. We're here to work, plain and simple. We're seasonal employees. It's the only way your mom would agree to take us—if she was sure we'd be out of her hair.

"This sucks." You throw your backpack on the ground, take a seat, pull out your water bottle, and drink the last of it. "We're going to die." You stare into the empty bottle.

I could tell you to stop being such a drama queen, but I know you need these little outbursts to keep yourself even, like how tiny earthquakes are supposed to be good for relieving pressure at fault lines. This is what you have to do to avoid The Big One. I hand you my water bottle. You drink, hand it back to me, sigh. Maybe you're right. Maybe we'll wander the cornfields for days until we die of dehydration, and the crows will feast upon our dried flesh, and when your mom finally remembers to pick us up, she'll find nothing but sun-bleached bones piled beside your fancy backpack and my beat-up suitcase.

"Ack!" You leap into the air and begin jumping like a crazy person.

"What?"

You point to something behind me. I spin around, follow your finger to a cloud of moving dust in the distance and what appears to be a truck in the middle of it. You jump and wave and try to make yourself as big as possible, as if you're afraid the driver won't see two brightly colored girls on the side of the empty road. I just stand there and watch the truck as it approaches. It's a beat-up old thing, and so is the man driving it. The truck slows to a stop, but you don't move toward it. For once you want me to do the talking. I approach the passenger's-side window. The wrinkled man is wearing a cowboy hat and denim overalls over a faded plaid button-up shirt, just like a movie farmer. He leans over and unrolls the window.

"Hello," I say, taking off my sunglasses.

"Are you girls lost?"

"No, sir," I say. "The bus from Omaha dropped us off out here and our ride didn't show up."

"Let me guess," he says. "You're one of them Oasis people."

"Oasis Farm! Yes, that's where we're going. Do you know how to get there?"

"Oh, sure," he says. He sighs, leans over again, and opens the door. "Get in. I'll give you girls a ride."

I run over and pull on your arm. "Come on," I say.

"Are you sure we should get in a car with him?" you whisper.

"He's just some old farmer," I say. "He's harmless."

"Max, he has a gun rack on his truck."

"It's for hunting, not for murdering people," I say. And I know it's a bad idea even before my mouth opens to form the words, but I say it anyway: "It's not like you've had a problem getting into cars with strange men before."

The sting washes across your face. Most things we can joke about with little snarky jabs. But some things still hurt too much. I should know that. I'm immediately sorry. I don't know why I said it. Maybe because you drank the last of my water. Maybe because I'm tired of sitting in the sun. The guilt wrenches through my guts.

You don't say anything, just pick up your backpack and walk toward the truck. "I'm sorry," I say, but you ignore me.

The man says "Throw your bags in the back." You get in first and I slide in next to you. The truck smells like menthol and vinyl.

"Hello," you say, again in your place as the one who handles things. "I'm Sadie."

"Mm-hmm," the man says, looking ahead as he starts driving.

"Do you know my mom, Lark Summerland? She lives at the Oasis Farm."

Something in his face twitches. "Can't say I know too many of them by name."

"Oh."

Still looking straight ahead, he says, "Young lady, you aware there's a spider crawling 'cross your forehead?"

You are all flailing arms and girl squeals. I think I see the slightest grin on the man's leathery face. "Get it off! Get it off!" you scream. You are slapping yourself in the face. I don't know why, but I pause before stopping you.

I catch your wrists, look into your wide eyes. "It's gone," I say.

"Where is it? Is it in my hair?" You break free from my grasp. "Oh, God! Is it in my hair?"

"Sit still," I command, and you obey, and I take a guilty pleasure in this rare moment when I can tell you what to do. I finger through your hair like the elementary school nurse used to do looking for lice. "You're good," I say, and you collapse onto my shoulder, take my hand in yours.

"Thank you," you sigh. "My savior." I feel a sparkle of pride and relief.

The man chuckles. "You girls are in for a treat," he says. The truck slows down and passes a faded wooden sign on the side of the road that reads Oasis Organic Farm. We turn down a narrow, potholed road lined with pink and purple bougainvillea, the first real color besides yellow, green, and blue it seems we've seen all day. A couple of mutts run alongside the truck, barking welcome. After a half mile or so, we pull into a large dirt circle flanked by old oak trees, some trucks, a house, a couple trailers, and what look like a few large tents, with more buildings and vehicles behind them. A larger Oasis Organic Farm sign greets us above a long raised bed of flowers and other plants. A few chickens wander the area, pecking at the dirt. This is the first real shade we've seen in hours, the first trees and buildings besides a couple of abandoned-looking tool sheds in the middle of vast lonely fields, and it does in fact feel like an oasis. The dogs circle the car, announcing us to whoever is here.

"Well, here you are," the man says.

"Thank you so much for the ride," you say.

"Mm-hmm."

I open the door, and we slide out, pull our bags from the back of the truck. You wave goodbye and yell "Thank you!" again, but there's no way he hears you over the sound of his truck rumbling away. We are left in a cloud of dust. The dogs approach, wagging their tails. One licks my hand.

"I hope these aren't supposed to be watchdogs," you say.

"Where is everyone?"

It is eerily quiet; the only sound is the slight rustling of leaves in the wind, the throaty clucking of the chickens, the friendly panting of the dogs. Then the sound of a screen door opening and springing closed. Booted footsteps on dirt. "Hello?" you say.

"Hello?" a man's voice responds. The dogs go running toward the voice, their tails wagging.

Your mom's boyfriend emerges from the side of the house. I recognize him from pictures you've shown me the last two years. You've never had much to say about him. He's a small man with a graying ponytail and the look of someone who's always slightly confused.

"Hi, Doff," you say.

He blinks, then smiles, then blinks again, says, "Shit, what time is it?"

Apparently the farm has one clock. A single clock. For the entire farm and all thirty-three, now thirty-five, people who live here. And it ran out of batteries. Nobody realized this until we showed up. Maybe they don't need clocks. Maybe they're those kind of people who are so attuned to nature they can tell what time it is by just looking at the sun.

"Your mom was supposed to pick you up," Doff says as we follow him into the house with our bags. "Everyone's still out in the field." We stop in the middle of a giant living room crowded with mismatched couches, chairs, and rugs, the walls covered with bookshelves and eclectic art. It is surprisingly cool inside, a rusty ceiling fan pushing the hot afternoon out the screen windows, a faint smell of earthy incense in the air. A computer that looks older than me sits on a small desk in the corner. The house is cozy in the way that basements or attics or tree houses are sometimes cozy, like the fact that most people would not choose to live there makes it that much more special.

"Does that thing work?" you ask, pointing at the ancient computer.

"Most of the time," Doff says. "We can't get DSL or cable out here, so it has to run on dial-up. It's pretty slow."

"What's dial-up?" you say.

Doff blinks. "I wonder where your mom is," he says, and keeps walking.

"Is this where we're staying?" I ask.

"In the house? No."

You look at me and raise your eyebrows. I shrug.

Doff walks us through the kitchen, pointing out the notorious clock on the wall that still reads 10:47. "Remind me to replace the batteries," he says. The walls are painted sunshine yellow, the cabinets an assortment of other bright colors. The air seems infused with the memory of hundreds of meals' worth of herbs and spices. Sliding glass doors reveal a large courtyard outside with several picnic tables. Like the living room, the kitchen is giant, with two stoves, two refrigerators, and two large metal sinks flanked by overflowing dish racks. The fridges are covered with the colorful, primitive art of children, the usual primary-color suns and trees and clouds. Instead of nuclear families, many of the drawings include innumerable stick figures attached at the hands like paper dolls.

"There are kids here?" you say.

"Oh yeah, a few. You'll meet them."

We look at each other again. You cross your eyes and stick your tongue out and I stifle a laugh.

"Is there anyone our age?" you ask.

"Well, there's Skyler. She's twelve. That's about the closest. Then the next closest I guess is Dylan. Not sure how old he is."

We see nothing but Doff's back as he slowly walks us through the house. All of his movements are slow and exaggerated, like he's moving through water. For a brief moment, I wonder if he's retarded. Either that or stoned.

"So, do you like living on a commune?" you say.

Doff stops and considers the question. "We prefer the term 'intentional community.'"

"What does that mean?" I hope he cannot hear the subtle teasing in your voice.

"Well, just what it says, really. That everything we do is intentional. We're here because we want to be. This is the life we choose and the people we choose to live it with. At least for now anyway."

I think there's something beautiful about this, something so simple and perfect—for a person to just leave the world they were given to create a new one they hope will be better. But you smirk and roll your eyes, and I know you think that Doff's a fool.

"Here are the showers," Doff says, motioning down a dark hall. I can make out three rickety-looking wooden stalls. "They can get pretty busy right around before dinnertime, after everyone comes in from working."

"Everyone shares these showers?" you ask, your face hinting at horror.

"Yep." Doff opens a door at the end of the hall and we step out onto a path that leads back to the shaded courtyard off the kitchen.

"Here's where we eat most of our meals. Except when the weather's bad. Then we have to stuff ourselves into the living room."

"Who does the cooking?"

Doff finally turns around, smiles in the confused way I am beginning to understand is his norm. "Well, *we* do, Sadie. We all do. We take turns doing everything."

We stand there for a moment, looking out past the

courtyard. In our few hours wandering the cornfields, I never would have guessed that something like this could be hidden within the flat, empty expanse of yellow. Rows of cabins, giant tents, and trailers stretch out on either side of the house, creating a horseshoe around a lake flanked by deep green grass and a scattering of huge trees. A tiny dock anchors a rowboat, and a half-deflated inner tube is stuck in a patch of reeds along the left shore. The afternoon sun glimmers on the surface of the lake, a family of ducks making lazy tracks through the water.

"It's beautiful," I say. Doff looks at me as if he forgot I was here.

"Can we swim in there?" you ask.

"Oh, sure," Doff says, his smile big. "We pull out all the algae and gunk from the bottom in the spring and use it for fertilizer. So the water's nice and clean and warm. And we got plenty of critters to keep the mosquitoes down."

"What kinds of critters?"

"Oh, we got some mosquitofish in there, and dragonflies and frogs love those cattails. Lots of birds and bats come by to visit."

"Bats?" You look scared.

"Don't worry, Sadie," Doff says. "They're just little guys. Not the vampire ones that suck your blood." Then he erupts in a shocking sound like a donkey honking, and I realize this must be his laugh. You giggle next to me, and then I start, and the day seems to just slide off around us and we start laughing in earnest. The dogs we met earlier come running, their faces stretched into comic grins. One leaps into the air and wraps his paws around your neck. You fall back, the dog on top of you, licking your face maniacally. You're laughing so hard you're crying, the way you do when I love you best. You flail on the ground as the dog wiggles on top of you.

"Che!" Doff shouts. "Off!"

"It's okay." You laugh, grabbing Che's muzzle and giving him a big kiss on the lips. "Who's this one?" you say, scratching the other one under the ear.

"That one's Biafra," Doff says. "They're drawn by laughter. It's the most peculiar thing. Whenever people laugh, they just come running. My laugh in particular." He makes the strange sound again and the dogs go ballistic, jumping at him and wagging their tails so fast it looks like they're going to take off.

"Oh my God," you pant as you pick yourself off the ground. "This is too much." I can't remember the last time I saw you this happy. I don't think we've laughed like this in months. A door inside me unlocks and creaks open, makes room for a little hope to seep in. Maybe this place will really change things. Maybe we can go back to the way it used to be, when we used to laugh all the time.

You wipe the tears from your face and we look out over the lake, at the fields of green rows beyond it. A few ant-sized people are walking in our direction. They wave. We wave back. As they get closer, I can start to make out each smiling, tanned face. I wonder why they have all chosen to live here. I wonder what it feels like to make a decision like that, to really *choose* a life, to not just do what's expected.

You step forward. I can feel you not breathing. A figure approaches, starts running, gets bigger and becomes your mother, as beautiful and long-legged as you, gracefully cutting through the air as she wraps her arms around you and you fall into her.

"Oh, my baby," she says. You bury your face in her long brown hair.

"Hi, Mommy," your baby voice says, and I can tell there are tears in your throat.

Your mom steps back and holds you by the shoulders, inspecting you. "You look like a flower!" she says, cupping the side of your face in one hand. She looks over at me and smiles. "And you must be Max."

"Hi," I say, and give a little wave.

"Oh, Max," she says, stepping in my direction. Her

smile has sunshine in it. "Thank you for being my daughter's friend." She puts her arms around me and squeezes for a long time, and I don't think I've ever gotten a hug like this from anyone besides you, not even my own family. She steps back and looks at us. "My girls for the summer," she says, and my heart jumps.

I look over at you, and your eyes are wet. We share a crinkly-eyed smile. I want to bottle up the hope and love in your face to show you later.

The others catch up and introduce themselves. I can't keep track of anyone's name, but I notice one has a long black beard and another has a faded tattoo of a peacock on his shoulder. I think one small man is either Japanese or Korean, and the woman who appears to be his mate is tall, thick, and Nordic looking. A pretty woman with hair down to her butt gives us both quick hugs and apologizes as she runs off, complaining of leaking breasts. A man I assume is her husband laughs at what must be the shock on our faces. "Time to breastfeed the baby," he explains.

"Oh," we say in unison.

After the marathon of introductions, everyone but Doff and your mom leaves, off to do whatever it is they do before dinner. Everyone we just met seemed so calm and friendly and warm—maybe they are onto something here; maybe they have found the secret to happiness. Maybe we will find it here too.

I turn to you, ready for you to share my enthusiasm. But before I have a chance to say anything, you scrunch up your face. "Everyone seems so *tired*," you whisper. "And dirty." I look at you, perplexed. "This is going to be awful," you proclaim clearly.

That is not what I was thinking. That is not what I was thinking at all.

Ἄρειος

WAR

The story of Troy was never about the wooden horse. That is only what people want to remember, something tangible and easy to imagine, something children can build with the popsicle sticks in their minds, then shove full of plastic warriors. The story people know goes like this: a gate, opened; the horse thrown inside; an explosion of violence accompanied by a soundtrack of killing, dying, and victory.

But the horse was only ever just a prop, something to hold the imagination, something simple to focus on instead of what the war, what any war, is really about. The horse was not full of soldiers but hopes and dreams and fears and secrets, all the things tucked inside the hearts of people who are lost. The story started long before that, with the gods and their eternal bickering, their jealousy and revenge and desire and all the other dysfunctions they passed onto their children, cursing man to a life of eternal wandering.

Heroes claim all sorts of things, but their journeys are never all that complicated. They pound their chests and show off their bloody trophies, but no one ever really remembers why they fight. They say it was about a woman, or land, or honor, or God, but in the end it is always about one thing—paradise—losing it and wanting it, finding it and defending it, and yearning, always yearning, for somewhere or something or someone that will make them feel whole.

Home. That is what the hero is always searching for. Sometimes other words are substituted. Love, for instance. Or God. But these are just other ways of saying "home."

"Let's show you to your new place, shall we?" your mom says, squeezing my shoulder. The dogs follow Doff toward the kitchen. He's on cooking duty for tonight's meal.

"Stay," Doff commands, but the dogs don't take him seriously, their tails wagging as they jump after him. "Stay!" he says again, and the dogs just seem to laugh at him by jumping higher.

"Che, Biafra," your mom says, her voice deep and forceful. "Stay!" And in a split second, the dogs sit down in unison. Doff looks at us with a sheepish grin, shrugs his shoulders, then turns around and continues toward the house.

"Alrighty," your mom says. "Off we go."

"Thank you so much," I say. "For letting me stay here this summer, Mrs. . . . um . . . Mrs.—"

"Oh, please." She rolls her eyes. "You can't be serious. *Mrs.*? Do I look like a *Mrs.* to you?" She starts leading us down a path away from the house. "My name is Lark," she says. "Nothing but Lark. Like Madonna, except aging gracefully."

I trail a few steps behind, giving you and Lark some space to catch up. But I need space too—just a few feet around me to breathe and take in my surreal surroundings. Just last night, I was hugging my dad goodbye and getting on a red-eye flight to Denver, asking him over and over again with rising panic in my voice if he was going to be okay without me, never believing him when he said yes. Is this how most teenagers react to spending a summer away from home? Is it normal to fear the world is going to fall apart without me? Is it normal for a seventeen-year-old girl to think her parents can't take care of themselves?

Now it's like I'm on a different planet. We've been deposited in this strange place where dogs are named after revolutionaries, where people live in tents, where mothers hug you every chance they can get. We're surrounded by unremarkable miles of corn, but here, hidden in plain sight, is this magical green place. You are glowing, like being near Lark has lit up some dormant place inside you, and maybe I don't have to worry about you anymore either. This is what I try to focus on—*your* happiness, *your* second chance—not the jealousy jabbing at my heart, not the yearning for my own mother, whose arms used to be as open as Lark's, whose love used to be that free, but who is now lost to me despite still living in my same house.

You always tell me I make things too complicated, I over-think everything, I am incapable of living in the moment. You told me this summer was going to be all about focusing on the *now*. It seems like it should be so easy, but I have to remind myself to feel the sun warming my skin, to smell the perfume of lavender in the air, to see my best friend in the whole world happy and calm and momentarily unwracked by the chaos that seems to follow you like a cloud. Yes, in this moment, right here and now, I think I'm happy too.

We make our way down the flower-lined path that leads to the right shore of the lake. It is dotted by a dozen or so dwellings, some sporting roofs of shiny solar panels. I would not call these "houses" necessarily; some are more like cabins, large enough to have one or two rooms; others are like big tents. There are potted plants and little rock paths, quite a few of those rainbow Tibetan prayer flags hanging, a few bicycles leaning here and there, toys strewn across the little front yards. One place has a whole flock of pink flamingos and a battered plastic Santa.

"That's Old Glen's place with the flamingos," Lark says.

"He's the one who started this place back in the eighties. Used to be a stockbroker on Wall Street. One day, he woke up and decided to just leave it all."

"Wow," I say.

"Wow is right. He's pretty amazing. Everyone here is, in one way or another."

I nod. You don't seem to have been listening. "Do any of these places have bathrooms?" you ask.

"There are composting toilets behind every three homes or so," Lark says. "But none of them has running water. We set up a water jug by each toilet for washing hands and stuff."

"What about electricity?"

"Oh yeah, everyone's got electricity." I'm pretty sure I hear you sigh in relief. "See those solar panels? This whole place is totally off the grid."

"So people live in these tents?"

"Oh, absolutely," Lark says. "They're called yurts. These are some of the nicest homes here. Very roomy."

"Even in the winter?" you ask in disbelief. This is probably as far as we could get from your dad's McMansion on the golf course. Or my less glamorous but just as cold house, where the TV's always on to cover up the silence.

"Honey, people have been living in places like this for thousands of years, through much crazier weather than we get here. Humans are capable of a lot more than they know." This strikes me as a strange thing to say in a conversation about architecture, but you just nod as if taking notes in your head.

We walk past a large yurt connected to a smaller one by a tentlike hallway. A little porch built off of the flap doorway holds a few chairs that face out toward the lake.

"That one looks like a hobbit house," you say.

"Who you calling a hobbit?" a man's low voice says behind us. I turn to see a jolly-looking man and a skeptical girl next to him. He's tall, with curly, graying shoulder-length hair, and she's pale and skinny, almost albino. They look nothing like hobbits.

"Marshall and Skyler!" Lark says. "It's your lucky day. Meet my beautiful girls, Sadie and Max."

"What an honor," Marshall says with an exaggerated bow. "Nice to meet you, ladies."

"You too," we say.

"This is my daughter, Skyler."

"Hi," we say. Skyler looks me quickly up and down and makes it clear with her arched eyebrow that she doesn't find much of interest. She's of that almost-pubescent age where her body is only slightly different from a boy's; her jean shorts and purple T-shirt are still from the kid's section.

"Skyler's twelve," Marshall says.

"Thirteen in three months," Skyler corrects him, but she's announcing it directly at you. As she attempts to transform from gawky girl to sassy almost-thirteen-year-old, she shifts her weight to one side, her hand going to her hip. She smiles hopefully and says, "I like your hair."

"Thanks," you say. "It's kind of washing out. It used to be a lot pinker."

"It's still really pink," Skyler says. "I was thinking of dyeing my hair pink too."

"No, you weren't," Marshall says. Lark and I make eye contact, and I catch her stifling a giggle.

"Dad, be quiet," Skyler says under her breath. "You don't know everything I think."

"Okay, Froggie. Whatever you say."

"Don't call me Froggie!" Skyler hisses, her freckled face turning red. "I already told you."

"Oh, pardon me," Marshall says with a fake British accent.

"Your yard is really pretty," I say. "I like the flowers." Skyler looks at me like I'm the twelve-year-old and she's the almost-senior in high school and I just said something really stupid.

"Thanks," Marshall says. "My wife's got a way with plants, for sure. Have you seen the veggies yet? She's kind of the plant whisperer of the farm." I shake my head no.

"They'll get the full tour Tuesday when they start work," Lark says. "They still haven't seen their trailer yet."

"Well, get along then," Marshall says. "Make yourselves at home. We'll see you at dinner."

"Bye, Sadie," Skyler says, then gives me the stink-eye.

"See ya," you say, but I can tell your mind is on something else. You must be just as terrified by the word "trailer" as I am.

Lark grins as she leads us. "I think someone's got a little crush on my daughter."

"Looks like it," I say. "Looked like she wanted to murder me in my sleep."

Lark gives me a surprised look. For a second, I wonder if I said something offensive, but then she breaks into a big laugh. "You're funny," she says. "I like you."

"I like you, too," I say, both confused and touched.

"Get a room," you joke, and we all laugh, and I can't help but imagine that I'm part of the family too, that Lark is our mom and you and I share the secret language of twins, and maybe we're not the orphans we always joke about being.

We get to a part of the path that seems to have been forgotten, as if no one ever walks this far. Weeds have broken through and nearly hide the gravel. Grass grows on either side as tall as our waists, with who knows what creatures hiding inside it. "Remember to check yourself for ticks on a regular basis," Lark says. I wait for her to add *Just kidding*, but she doesn't. We turn the corner past a little grove of trees, and the buzzing of insects gets louder.

Around the corner sits a rusty old trailer, the kind of giant tin can people attach to the back of a truck. It looks like it's been sitting here since before we were born. As we approach and Lark moves to open the door, I fully expect squirrels or birds to fly out, rabid raccoons and rats. The joy I felt only minutes before suddenly begins to sour. I reach over and lightly touch your wrist. You touch mine back, and I know you are thinking the same thing.

This is the end of the road. The overgrown path stops at a pile of bricks that have been stacked to make a step to the trailer's front door. The trees cast the scene in shade, the tall grass rustling its creepy soundtrack. The yurts are starting to look nice.

"You girls should see the looks on your faces," Lark says with a chuckle. "Don't freak out. We didn't get a chance to mow around it. That can be your first job tomorrow. But the inside is lovely, trust me."

Lark opens the door and I hold my breath as we peer inside. I don't know what I expect—torn velvet paintings on the walls, stained linoleum, a meth lab?—but that is not what I see. The inside is indeed lovely—it is painted a cheerful peach with little framed paintings dotting the walls and Christmas lights hanging from the ceiling. Two twin beds are snug at one end, covered by homemade quilts and nests of mismatched pillows, a soft blue curtain tied to the side to separate the sleeping area from the other half of the space. Old Oriental rugs line the floor past a closet and dresser to the other end of the trailer, where bookshelves have been built on top of the nonfunctioning sink and stove, and a love seat and beanbag chair make a cozy nook.

Lark takes one look at us and says, "Now, that's the reaction I was looking for."

"Oh, Mom," you say breathlessly. "It's beautiful."

"I'm so glad you like it, sweetie."

"It's like the best clubhouse ever," I add.

Lark's eyes are all smile lines and warmth. "I'm so glad you're here."

"Me too," we say at the same time, and it feels like I've never meant anything more in my life. This is so the opposite of back home. Lark is so the opposite of the ghost my mother has become. This place is nothing like anything I wanted to get away from.

Νηρηίς

NEREIDS

They were goddesses and women and rivers and lakes. They were maybe even a little bit fish, a little bit water bug or otter, or some other live, swimming thing. It was impossible to tell where their bodies stopped and the water started, where warm flesh gave way to cool liquid. It was in their blood, this water, all the particles and bubbles and memories, pulsing inside them and giving them breath.

A wave could be her hip, her breast, the curve of her shoulder. And on a hot day, you might think she's salvation. You're delirious with thirst, almost blind, but you can make out her lips and their promise of wetness; her long thin fingers weaving you like pond grass, making a basket of your desire. So you follow her in, led underwater by this creature who is always out of reach—part water, part woman—translucent, glimmering. And she takes you down deep, to the place where only mud and shadow live, where she is only darkness, only a hand holding you under.

As soon as we set our bags down in the trailer, you break into tears and throw yourself at your mother. I wonder if she knows this about you, that you do this kind of thing. I wonder if she knows how overcome you get. There is no consoling you when you're like this, but Lark seems like an expert, patiently patting you on the back until the storm subsides. After a few minutes of wailing, your tiny earthquake is over. You lift your head, your face puffed red and slimy with snot and tears, your hair like a punk rock Medusa's, and you sniffle. "Sorry, guys, I just needed to get that out." You get up and take your boots off, wiggle your toes a little, walk calmly out the door, and proceed to undress while walking the ten or so yards to the lake. A trail of socks, leggings, and sundress marks your path. You stand at the edge of the lake in your underwear and bra and lift your arms high in the air, your body elongating into a beautiful taut thing, the ripples of your ribs like piano keys.

It is times like these when I'm struck dumb by your beauty and simultaneously surprised that I have never once felt the slightest attraction to you. I have wanted to kiss lots of girls, and you are by far the most beautiful girl I've ever known, but I have never wanted to kiss you. Maybe it's because you're less a girl and more like something else, something that straddles the worlds of light and dark, something only half here, something half untouchable.

Lark and I stand side by side in the doorway of the trailer. As I look out from the shade, the sun seems extra golden, like a giant spotlight for this world that is your stage, as if this lake is the source of all your power. You turn around and wave at us, smile, then dive into the water.

"Oh my God!" you yell when you surface. "This feels amazing."

"Go," Lark says, poking me in the ribs. "Looks like you need a splash after your travels."

I strip down to my underwear and bra and join you in the water. It is the perfect temperature—cold enough to be refreshing, but warm enough so a person could stay in it all day if they wanted. I grab you by the waist and pull you under. We wrestle, taking turns dunking each other and surfacing to laugh and breathe.

When we get back to the trailer, we are breathless and dripping wet. Lark is gone.

I peel off my bra and underwear as a pool of water forms at my feet. "Guess we'll have to drip dry," I say. You don't hear me. You are busy peering out each of the trailer's three small windows. You even open the tiny closet. You are looking for her.

"She probably had to do something to get ready for dinner," I say.

You don't say anything, just open your backpack and start putting your things in the dresser. "We have to remember to ask someone for towels," I say. You nod and continue unpacking.

"Talk to me, Sadie," I say. Finally, you look up, give me a weak smile.

"It's been a long day," you say.

"Yes, it has."

"I think I'm about to start my period."

"Oh." And I understand that this is going to be the extent of your explanation for shutting me out. I let it go like I always do.

We manage to air dry and put on clothes. We unpack all our stuff. You get the top two drawers, and I get the bottom; you get the left side of the closet, I get the right. We bravely venture out back to the toilet, which is a wooden shed with a toilet seat on top of bench over a hole in the ground. There's a bucket of sawdust and one with some sort of white powder. And toilet paper. Thank God, at least there's toilet paper.

"I guess you're supposed to put those in there?" you say, pointing from the buckets to the toilet.

I nod in agreement. "To cover up your business." We are already becoming experts in off-the-grid living.

We open all the drawers and cabinets in the trailer, read the spines of the books in the little library. Most of them are old yellowed paperbacks of titles I don't recognize, but there are some familiar names like Tom Robbins, Jack Kerouac, and Ken Kesey, a couple of books about Buddhism, Sufism, environmentalism, feminism, and 1960s history. "It's like the suggested reading list for Hippies 101," you say, and that cracks us up for a while. I find an old glass jar in one of the cabinets, and we pick wildflowers to put on the little coffee table between the love seat and beanbag chair. I already know that the love seat will be your official spot for the summer, that you will claim it with your long body draped across it—one side under your calves and the other propping up the pillow to cushion your head—and I will be relegated to the beanbag chair on the floor. It is only natural—I am the more compact and self-contained of us, and you are the one who needs to spread out.

Just when I am starting to feel my stomach growling, we hear a little knock on the side of the trailer, then see Skyler peering through the screen door.

"Hello?" she squeaks.

"Hi," you say, lifting yourself up to stretch and yawn. "Come on in."

Skyler opens the screen door a crack. "I'm supposed to tell you it's almost time for dinner." Just then, we hear a bell ring a few times from the direction of the main house. "That's what that bell means."

"I'm starving!" you say, jumping off the couch. I pull myself up from the beanbag and feel my body ache in unfamiliar places. I feel creaky already, and we haven't even started working.

We follow Skyler up the path to the main house. The other side of the lake is like a reflection of ours, a waterfront row of yurts and cabins and trailers with people spilling out on the way to dinner.

"Your place is nice," Skyler says. "I helped paint it."

"Thank you," you say. "I love the color."

"I picked it out," Skyler says proudly.

We're the last ones to get to the house. Everyone's lining up with plates and making their way through the kitchen where Doff and a few others serve food. I notice your eyes darting around, no doubt searching for Lark. Skyler hands us plates from a pile by the door, and we stand there, inching our way forward as the line advances. I know there are only a little more than thirty people living here, but it seems like a million faces with a million different smiles, so many people my parents' age who look and act nothing like my parents. Most of the men have some form of facial hair and none of the women wear makeup; everyone is tan and bright-eyed, and apparently hugging is big here. My body tenses as another stranger throws her arms around me, but you act like a natural, melting into each one of them like they're family, even as you roll your eyes behind their backs. Little kids run around between people's legs, and no one yells at them to calm down. The room is so full of life it makes me dizzy.

I think I was expecting everyone to be younger, like in photos of sexy, half-naked twenty-year-olds during the Summer of Love, with Lark and Doff just being the old-people exceptions. But I'd say most of the adults here are in their forties, some even older. They're actual grown-ups, but they live in tents and poop in holes and eat food they grow with their own hands, and maybe this is as grown-up as they ever want to get.

My mind is totally blown.

We wait our turns to be served, and I'm not sure what much of it is, but all of it is colorful. There's some green leafy thing and some brown rice with various-colored vegetables mixed in and some kind of very tender meat. Doff tops it all off with a deep red sauce and asks us how we like the trailer. We tell him it's beautiful, the lake is beautiful, the trees are beautiful, the food is beautiful, everything is so freaking beautiful.

Everyone is sitting at the outdoor picnic tables. Marshall calls Skyler over, and she sulks off to sit with her family. You look around for Lark but she's still missing. We take the last empty bench across from the pretty woman with leaking breasts and her black-bearded husband, whose names we learn are Maria and Joseph.

"No way!" you say. "Is your baby named Jesus?"

"Nothing that interesting," Maria laughs. "Just Patrick. But we call him Bean." Little Bean is attached to Maria's uncovered boob, and it takes all my strength not to stare.

An old man stands up at the front edge of the courtyard, with the sunlit lake and houses and fields glowing behind him. The sun catches the wisps of his gray hair and forms a halo around him. "That's Old Glen," Joseph says. "He likes to make speeches."

Old Glen clears his throat, and everyone quiets. "Let us

thank Geraldine, Doff, Sarah, Ben, and Ezra for tonight's delicious food." Everyone says "Thank you" in unison, and my inner *is this a cult?* alarm goes off a little. Old Glen continues, "Let us thank the plants and grains and especially Jimbo, who gave his life so that we could eat meat on this special night." Everyone says "Thank you" again, and I look down at the piece of meat lying on my plate. I turn my head to see you doing the same thing. Our eyes meet and you mouth *Jimbo?* I giggle, but you look horrified.

"But the biggest news of the evening, as everyone knows," Old Glen says, "is the arrival of our special summer guests who are joining our big family." Every single face, all sixty-plus eyes, turn in our direction. "Let us all say 'Welcome.'"

And they all say "Welcome" in unison, and they clap, and I don't think I've ever had this many people looking at me at once in my entire life. Maria reaches over and squeezes my hand. I shrink and shrivel with the attention, while you seem to absorb it and get even bigger and brighter than you already were.

"We are so happy to welcome Lark's daughter, Sadie, and her friend Max to our community, and I know you will all do your best to make them feel welcome." You give a little wave like you're accepting an award. I know my face is beet red as I try to smile in your shadow.

Old Glen says a little more, listing off everyone's work

duties for tomorrow—jobs like planting, weeding and harvesting specific vegetables, building fences, turning compost, milking cows, and other farm duties. There are also tasks like child care, meal prep and cleanup, driving to town for supplies, and cleaning the main house and showers. Everyone nods when their name is called; no one seems surprised or disappointed by their assignment. A few people have days off, including us.

I had no idea a commune would be so organized. I had imagined a world without rules, an anarchic paradise where people would run around doing whatever they wanted and somehow the work would magically get done. But I guess it makes sense that a working farm needs some kind of leadership, and I guess it makes sense that their leader would be the guy who founded it. I wonder if Old Glen is the one who decides all the job assignments, or if people have a say in what they do. Does everyone have to do everything equally, regardless of whether or not they like it or are any good at it? Maybe part of the freedom here is not having to make any decisions. Maybe everything is randomly assigned, or maybe Old Glen decides everything for everyone. I wonder which freedom is more free—freedom to make any decision you want, or freedom from having to make any at all.

Lark appears at the other end of the patio, talking to

Marshall. You wave frantically in her direction until you catch her eye, and she comes over, wraps her arms around us.

"I saved you a seat," you say, but Lark just hovers, says she's on cleanup duty tonight and has to get to work soon. You say, "Okay," cheerfully, and I'm the only one trained to notice the almost imperceptible disappointment on your face.

Everyone is eating and talking, and I'm watching birds fishing in the lake, diving down and disappearing for a few moments, then rising again, sometimes with food, sometimes not. I don't know what it is that affects their chances, why some dives are successful and others not. I wonder if they even know, if they can reflect on their attempts and learn from mistakes, adjust and do better next time. Or maybe they're not that smart. Maybe they think it's all based on luck—some birds have it, some don't—and it's not up to them whether or not they succeed, not up to their talent or hard work or dedication to the task; maybe it's just an arbitrary decision made by some mysterious gods. And they keep going through the motions imprinted in their blood, waiting for the gods to smile on them.

I am suddenly very tired, and I don't think I will be able to wait for the sun to go down to sleep. I notice you picking at the food around Jimbo as you chat with the man with the shoulder tattoo we met earlier.

"Nice peacock," you tell him.

"It's not a peacock," he says with a mouth full of food. "It's a phoenix. You must know about phoenixes."

"Like in Harry Potter?" you say.

"Harry who?" the man says. We look at each other in disbelief. Has this guy been living under a rock?

"A phoenix is a very powerful mythical creature," he says earnestly. "It symbolizes rebirth. A phoenix burns, then rebuilds itself from its ashes. It's very poetic," he says, taking another large bite of food. A few crumbs fall out of his mouth. I notice he has a slight twitch in his left eye. Up close, maybe not everyone here is as beautiful as they seemed at first.

Lark has disappeared again, and Skyler is staring at you from across the patio like a psychopath, and despite the giant boom of "Welcome," despite all these people's friendly smiles and conversation, I suddenly feel as lonely as I do at home with the silence, with the specter of my mother lost inside herself.

I look around and watch the families here, the mothers and fathers eating with their children, the other couples leaning into each other. I spot Lark wrapping her arms around Doff from behind, see him rest his cheek on her arm and close his eyes, see her kiss the top of his head. I feel an ache inside, and I can't distinguish its point of view, if I'm yearning for parents like these, or yearning to be one of the couples, yearning to be someone in love. Maybe both, maybe neither, but I am doing that thing I always do—the obsessing about what I don't have, the ignoring where I am right now.

So I do the exercise you taught me, one you learned from the therapist you've been seeing since you were seven. I close my eyes, count from one to five as I breathe in slowly, count backward from five to one as I breathe out. I do this a few times until my heart stops aching so sharply and I forget what I was thinking about. Maybe relaxation is just forgetting what you're supposed to be worried about.

When I open my eyes, I am disoriented. I focus on someone new, someone I haven't seen before, sitting in the corner, leaning back in his chair like he knows something the rest of us don't. His dark hair is messy and hiding half his face. His jeans are dark and his T-shirt is black and his arms are half covered with tattoos. My eyes meet his and I suddenly forget how to breathe; I feel the courtyard whoosh close around me, and everything in my body burns and feels numb at the same time.

"That's Dylan," Skyler says behind me, making me jump. She has momentarily escaped the table with her parents and has come back to torture me. "He's too old for you."

I look at you, and your face is turned in the same direction. You are oblivious to both Skyler and me. You have the same hungry look on your face I must have had on mine.

ἄρμα

LOVE

Once upon a time, you would not have recognized us. *People were not people but big fleshy boulders, with two sets each of hands and legs and fingers and toes, one head on top with two faces looking in opposite directions. It was not a pretty sight, these human balls, but they were happy, whole, rolling around wherever they pleased. If they found a long straight road, and especially if it started at a bit of an incline, they could get going so fast they could change the molecules in the air; they could burn the grass into crispy tendrils, turn sand into glass, melt rocks into magma.*

The Sun is a man. His sons were hairier than the rest and slightly more muscular. They were stubborn and less adept at multi-tasking. They rumbled and belched when they rolled.

The Moon is a woman. Everyone knows this. When her daughters sang, the oceans moved. Their flesh was soft, and when they rolled they liked to know where they were going.

But the Earth, she is a fickle thing. He is full of tides and plates and seasons and volcanoes, the constant flow of water and earth, part Sun and part Moon, always. He is both male and female, and her offspring were the same—one face mustached and low-voiced, the other smooth with heart-shaped lips; two arms thick and tight, two arms long and graceful. You looked at one face and perhaps she was smiling, but then you turned her around and he was frowning on the other side. But the sadness was only shallow and soon passed. They did not know true sadness, for they were never alone.

We must not forget the gods and their jealous insecurities. We must not forget how power corrupts, how it craves itself, how it chases its tail like Ouroboros. There was something threatening about these eight-limbed creatures, something great and powerful. Their completeness was something even the gods didn't have, and these children of flesh were prideful. They forgot their place. They thought they had a right to heaven.

This is the downside of being complete. Others want what you have. They covet your doneness.

So the gods, in their epic tantrum, threw thunderbolts and cut each ball right down the middle. Each cut was its own snow-flake, a surgical fingerprint; no two were alike. The balls became sad crescents—the Moon only half full, the Sun eclipsed, the Earth with a big bite taken out of it. Those who once rolled so gracefully became wobbly upright creatures who had to learn how to walk on two legs like toddlers. They were stretched and turned like gro-tesque clay, their heads spun around to face forward, their gaping wound pulled shut and tied at the belly button. They were shaped like fleshy stars.

And so love was born. The once-complete creature became two incomplete halves. Out of the pain of being separated came the yearning to be whole, to be reunited with that single lonely crea-ture whose jagged edges are an exact mirror image of our own.

"We've got work to do," you announce, pulling on shorts and a tank top. It is early, too early. But right away, I can tell you're on a mission. And there's no stopping you when you're on a mission.

"What about breakfast?" I say.

"We'll grab it on our way."

"On our way where?"

"To get tools."

You are normally not an early riser. But here, maybe you will be someone else.

When we get to the courtyard we find that everyone is already out in the fields working. The only people left are Maria and another woman on child-care duty for the day, one man tidying up in the kitchen, plus the half-dozen children of the farm, who are busy drawing at the picnic tables. Both women are breastfeeding, Maria with Bean attached to her chest, the other with a much older child. I know I met the woman yesterday, but it's all a blur and I can't for the life of me remember her name.

"I don't think that's her kid she's feeding," you whisper. The woman is white, and the child at her breast is many shades darker.

"Maybe the father's black," I offer.

"I don't think so," you say. "Did you see any black guys here?"

"Maybe he's not here," I say. "Maybe they broke up."

You look at me skeptically. "How *old* is that kid, anyway? He can definitely talk. Do you think he just goes *Hey, Mom, give me your boob* when he's hungry?"

I shrug. You shudder. "It's so gross," you say. "To breastfeed a kid that old." *According to whom?* I want to say. *What makes you such an expert?* I'm not sure where this spurt of anger comes from. Maybe I'm grumpy from being woken up so early.

Maria grins big when she sees us and motions us to come over. I start moving in her direction, but you grab my arm. "No time, Max," you say so only I can hear. A couple of the kids look up at us curiously, then return their attention to their drawings.

"Later," I shout over to her. "We're in a hurry. We have a lot to do today." You smile a big fake smile as you pull me away. You're the one who decides we can't talk, but I'm the one who has to worry about being rude.

"Okay," Maria says back. "Let me know if you need any help. The kids can help too. Right, kids?"

They all look up and nod yes. A little boy around four or five demands in a squeaky voice, "Do you know why the Lorax is sad?"

"Oh," I say. "Um. I forget. Why?"

"Because corporations keep cutting down trees to make freeways," he lectures. "And genetic engineerings and the bad guy named Monsanto makes fish with three eyeballs."

You guffaw behind me. I can't help but smile. "I don't remember that part of the Lorax," I say.

Maria laughs. "I think River might have gotten a few things mixed up."

"But he's basically on the right track," the other woman says. "Dr. Seuss was a revolutionary, you know. Seriously subversive." Maria nods like this is common knowledge.

"Come on," you hiss, and I let you drag me away.

You instruct me to make peanut butter sandwiches. You

find apples, carrots. We throw our peasant meal into a canvas bag you discover shoved in a corner. The clock on the wall still reads 10:47.

"What about coffee?" I ask.

"No time for coffee."

You're the foreman of our operation, and I am the worker you picked up on the side of the road by Home Depot. You give me instructions, and I obey, nodding yes and saying little. Carry this WeedWacker, grab that plastic chair, those milk crates, that board, this pink flamingo, that flower pot, this little broken figurine of an owl. We raid the garage for anything useful we can find.

I chop the waist-high grass around the trailer with the WeedWacker, and you follow with the mower. Seeds and grass fly through the air and stick to the glue that is our sweat, get tangled in the Velcro that is our hair. We become one with the heat and the stickiness and the itch. When we are half done, we take a water-and-peanut-butter-sandwich break.

"This is our initiation," you say, picking something that looks like wheat out of your hair. Your skin is already bronzing. You are already becoming part of the sun.

"Initiation into what?"

"Our summer of hard labor."

The sun is almost directly above us in the sky. Sometime somewhere, I learned that this means noon. We get back to work.

We tame our new home. We soften all signs of neglect. We mow the grass until it's flat and uniform, and we build a table out of milk crates and abandoned wood. The plastic chairs wobble, but they're not too bad. As we sit eating the last of our food, surveying our day of work, you've got a satisfied look on your face. I can hear you crunching an apple, and the sound comforts me. The birds accompany you with their music. The leaves rustle harmonies.

"Did you see that woman's armpit hair?" you say.

"What woman?"

"The one breastfeeding that toddler. It was as long as the hair on my head."

"But not pink, I hope."

"No, not pink," you say. "That would be *unnatural*. That would, like, offend the Earth Mother Goddess or some shit." You laugh at your own joke. I look across the lake, at the other side so eerily empty.

"Max," you say seriously. You look at me, raise your eyebrows, stop chewing. I already know what you're thinking. "*That guy.* At dinner last night. Sitting in the corner."

"I know."

"He was beautiful."

"Very."

"How old do you think he is?"

"I don't know. Maybe twenty? Twenty-two? Skyler says he's too old for us."

"She said he's too old for *you*."

"But I'm older than you."

"Only by seven days."

"Whatever," I say.

"Time to swim," you say. "Let's get our suits on."

So we do, our motions matched and fluid. From far away, I imagine someone might think we're twins. Since we were little, teachers have always said *Those two are attached at the hip*, and I've taken it as a source of pride.

We have always understood that our relationship comes first. There have been a fair share of romantic sides, most of them yours, but none ever lasts too long. You always stay true, rarely even sleeping with the same boy twice. Most would think of this as problematic; they do not know you're being faithful to me. For you, there is a difference between sex and love. And what we have is love. The rest is simply entertainment.

Perhaps it is harder for me, my attractions being more ambiguous. You can safely say boys on one side, Max on the other. The line is straight and sharp. But mine curves all around; everything is gray instead of black and white.

I thought I was in love once. I never told you this. I knew it would break your heart. I let you think the relationship was something less, something like all of yours. By then, I had only a few kisses, a couple make-out sessions, and one awkward virginity loss with Hans, that German exchange student sophomore year. But then I met Elka, and at first I tried to pretend it was just a fling. I reported our trysts to you, doing my best to imitate your carelessness. You'd laugh and call me a slut, and I knew you were proud of me. But then I found there were things I didn't want to share, things I wanted to be just mine. Like the way Elka would cup my chin in her hand when she thought I said something cute, the way she'd always rest her head on my shoulder when we watched movies, the way we'd breathe in each others' breath when we kissed.

I don't blame you for our breakup. I know it wasn't meant to last. Elka was on her way somewhere dark and I didn't want to go along for the ride. Not like with you. Your darkness is familiar. Your darkness I'm good at handling. But I sometimes wonder what would have happened if I stayed with her. What if the drugs were just a phase she would snap out of soon, and I'd have her back the way I wanted? Sometimes I wonder if things weren't as bad as you eventually convinced me they were, if maybe your jealousy was more at play than concern for me. But this thought never lasts for long. I know you love me more than anyone in the world, more than Elka ever would have, even if she could stay sober. I must remember this. Above all else, this is what's important. Girlfriends and boyfriends will come and go, but you will always be my constant.

We float. I practice stillness. I feel the breeze's gentle nudges toward the shore. When I get too close, I flap my hands like lazy fins, and I move back toward the center of the lake. I try not to imagine what might be under me, what dark and hiding things are slithering where I can't see them. You don't seem afraid. The water is an extension of you. I think I hear your voice in the song it makes. You are floating in the corner of my eye, your face tilted toward the sun and a gentle smile on your face, and I think there must be nothing in your head but this water, this single place in time. This is your gift, this miraculous ability to just *be* wherever you are. You are weightless in more ways than one. The best I can do is float on this water while all the thoughts in my head threaten to drown me.

You float, serene, while I am the one burdened with memories. I have the job of holding on to your history, our history. I'm the one who remembers why we are here. I'm the one who has to be scared. You do not question the logic of paying a homeless guy to buy you whiskey. You do not question the idea of two teenage girls wandering around Seattle at night with the bottle in a paper bag, you taking five gulps for every one of my sips. I always know you're getting drunk when your arms start waving in the air when you talk, the way you make yourself bigger the less sense you make. It's when I'm ready to stop that you're just getting started.

Men are drawn to drunk girls. They have a sixth sense that alerts them when a girl somewhere reaches the point where she's incapable of making conscious decisions, when she has no one to protect her but a wimpy best friend. When you stumbled and fell slow-motion to the pavement, three chunky frat boys miraculously appeared to catch you. You laughed as they helped you back on the sidewalk. You thanked them even though I knew you couldn't see them, even though your eyes couldn't focus. You didn't notice when one of the boys' hands squeezed your breast unnecessarily, or when the other two shared a knowing smirk.

"Sadie, let's go," I said.

"Where are you girls going?" one said.

"We're going home."

"Oh, Max," you slurred. You giggled as you leaned against one of the boys, as his big fat hand snuck its way under your shirt.

"Sadie, let's go," I said, pulling on your arm. They were not butterflies in my stomach, but bees, wasps, hornets, fierce and stinging.

"We'll give you a ride," one said. They all looked the same. "Our car is right around the corner." He pulled keys out of his pocket, jangled them like a cat toy, and you grabbed at them, purring.

"Let me drive!" You laughed, and the boys laughed. The one with the keys mumbled to another that he was going to get the car. Something sharp tore through my whiskey haze, something barbed and hot and terrifying.

"Sadie, we have to go," I said. "We have to go *right now*."

"We're getting a ride," you said. "We don't have to take the bus, Max!" You announced this so proudly, like you had found us a great deal. The boy propping you up had his hand fully under your shirt now. I could see it moving around, like some kind of alien disease. He was grinning at me with droopy eyes.

A car pulled up. The boy leaned out the window. "Get in," he said. Something loud and ugly was blaring from the stereo, the kind of music frat boys listen to so they can pretend they have something to be angry about.

I said, "No." You said nothing. You got in the car, and it drove away before you even had a chance to close the door.

I stood there on the curb as the music faded away. "Oh my God," I remember saying aloud, to no one. The street was empty. No one saw. You were gone. You were drunk, and you were in a car with three strangers. And it was my fault. It is my job to keep you safe, and I let them take you.

My hand was shaking as I called everyone I could think of. I called your dad, but he didn't answer. I called my house. I even called Elka, even though we had broken up two months earlier and weren't speaking. I didn't leave any messages; I couldn't commit any words to being saved for later, couldn't take on the responsibility of defining what was happening. Anything could have been happening to you, but I was still worried about getting you in trouble.

I had drunk a fair share of that whiskey bottle, but I had never felt more sober in my life. I felt the crisp night air taking bites out of my skin, saw every city light burning, cruel and menacing. It was the end of the world. I was not breathing. I did not deserve to breathe. I had lost you.

I thought I was dreaming when I heard music again in the distance. The screech of tires as the car turned the corner is what finally convinced me it was real; this was really the car driving toward me, this was really me running toward it and yanking the back door open; this was really you falling out and onto the curb, your mascara smeared down your face and the neck of your shirt ripped; this was me screaming something into the night air, not English, not even language; this was me scooping you into my arms; this was some asshole muttering "crazy bitch" as the car drove away, taking the angry music along with it, along with the boys who have absolutely nothing in this world to be angry about.

"What happened?" I screamed as you wept. You shook your head no. I searched your body for signs, for answers. "What did they do?"

"Nothing," you whimpered.

"Sadie, what did they do?"

"Nothing!" You broke free of my arms and stood up on your wobbly legs. You started walking.

"Where are you going?"

"I have to find a bathroom."

"We have to go home, Sadie."

You kept walking.

"I'll call a cab," I said. But I didn't call anyone. I didn't even take out my phone. I just followed you across the street and around the corner. I followed you as you walked toward the dirty neon sign of a windowless bar. "Sadie," I said. "You can't go in there."

Old men sat on bar stools watching a dingy TV in the corner. It looked like they had been there for years. All heads turned when we burst through the door. The bartender said, "Hey, I need to see some ID," but you veered toward the bathroom sign. "Hey," the bartender said again.

"She just has to use the bathroom," I said, and followed you in.

You climbed onto the counter, lodged yourself in the corner against the wall, and puked in the sink. The already rancid bathroom filled with smells of whiskey and sadness and half-digested dinner. I tried running the faucet but it wouldn't go down.

"Fuck, Sadie!" I said.

"Fuck Sadie, fuck Sadie, fuck Sadie," you cried in response. Your arms hugged your knees against your chest as you rocked back and forth. "Fuck fuck fuck fuck." You threw up again.

The bartender pounded on the door. "What are you girls doing in there?"

"My friend's sick," I said.

"You get out of there or I'm going to call the cops."

"Come on, Sadie," I said. You shook your head. Your eyes were closed, and they would not be opening for a long time.

"Come on!"

"I'm calling the cops right now," the bartender said.

"No, wait," I said, but he was already gone. I tried pulling you off the counter, but you wouldn't budge. I tried explaining what was happening so you would understand, but all you did was shake your head. I tried asking you what you were thinking, but you were gone. All I could do was hold your hair and wait for whatever was going to happen.

There was a strange kind of stillness in those moments before the cops arrived. I think it's possible to be filled with so much worry that fear takes a person full circle to where they reach this saturation point where nothing matters any more. I was worried about what happened to you in the car, worried about the cops, worried about our parents, so worried about everything that I was just numb. The world was so big and heavy around me that it couldn't even start to fit in my head. There was only this bathroom and the buzz of fluorescent lights. There was the feeling of your hair in my hands, the smell of your insides. There was only this moment, and I was nowhere else. It was the closest to Zen I think I have ever felt.

But then the paramedics arrived with their stethoscopes and questions, their efficient kindness. A female medic told everyone but me to get out, so it was just the three of us in the dirty bathroom. She shined a tiny flashlight in your eyes and asked you how you were doing. "I'm okay," you said in a little girl voice. "Are you going to take me home?"

"What's she on?" the woman asked.

"Just whiskey," I said.

"I need you to tell me everything she took tonight."

"Just whiskey, I swear." But maybe not. Maybe you took something else. Maybe the boys gave you something in the car.

"This is Max," you said, your eyes still closed. "She's my

best friend. She saved me." Your shoulders shook with sobs and tears seeped out from under your closed lids.

"Well, that was nice of her," the paramedic said, unmoved.

Someone knocked on the door.

"This is Officer Myers," a man's voice said. "Can I come in?"

"Give us a second," the paramedic said, then I swear she mumbled "fucking cops" under her breath. "What's your name, sweetheart?" she said gently, holding your face up. You opened your mouth, but nothing came out.

"Sadie," I answered for you.

"Sadie, you don't want to do this kind of thing anymore, do you?"

"What thing?" you said as your head dropped back down.

"Getting in trouble like this," the paramedic said. "This isn't the kind of girl you want to be, is it?"

You shook your head no. Tears splashed around you.

"I'm going to talk to the officer outside for a second while your friend gets you cleaned up, okay?"

"Okay."

"You're too young for this shit."

"Okay."

"Say it," the paramedic said. "Say 'I'm too young for this shit.'"

You mumbled something that sounded reasonably similar.

The paramedic looked at me sternly before she left to talk to the officer, one more person agreeing that this was somehow my fault.

"Are you okay?" I asked. You nodded. "Are you ready to go home?"

"We're in trouble," you said, suddenly coherent.

"Yes, we are."

"I'm sorry," you said. I could tell you were trying to open your eyes.

"I know."

"I love you, Max," you said.

"I know, Sadie."

"You love me too."

"Yes."

"Say it. Say you love me too."

"I love you, Sadie. I love you more that anything in the world."

The paramedic returned. "I convinced Officer Myers not to write you up this time," she said. "You girls are really fucking lucky."

"Thank you," I said. "Thank you so much."

"He is going to drive you home, though," she continued. "And he's going to talk to your parents, young lady," she said, putting her hand on your arm. I remember a sudden and blinding jealousy. I wanted her hand on *my* arm; I wanted a kind stranger to comfort *me* for once. And then an instant shame like a slap in the face. My best friend was about to be taken home by the cops, and I was worried about what *I* wanted.

The back of the police car was dark and smelled like disinfectant. The molded plastic seat was hard and cold. Officer Myers lectured us the whole way home through the clear window that separated the good guys in the front from the bad guys in the back. You were passed out, so I was the one who had to listen to his cautionary tales of all the bad things that can happen to drunk girls in the city. It was nothing I hadn't heard before. Every story he told starred you in my mind, running blind, flailing around and knocking things over, and I was always scrambling behind you trying to pick up the broken pieces.

I got dropped off first. I gave the officer your address. He didn't bother walking me to the door or talking to my parents, like he had already decided I wasn't worth the trouble. I was supposed to spend the night at your place, so no one was expecting me home. No lights were on. I let myself in with no one noticing. I watched the cop car drive away with you sleeping soundly in the back seat like you had no idea anything was wrong. I slept well that night, not only because

I was exhausted, but because I knew you were at least safe for the night and I didn't have to take care of you.

You texted me the next day: *My dad's sending me to live in Nebraska for the summer!*

Nebraska?! I responded.

It's good news! you wrote. *I'm going to live with my mom!*

You had been trying to convince Lark to take you for years. You finally got your wish. All it took was drinking yourself stupid, getting kidnapped by three assholes, puking in a bar sink, and almost getting arrested.

She said you can come too!! So many exclamation points for someone who spent so much of last night puking. *Ask your parents!*

So I did. And they said yes. And that was that. Two teenage girls shipped off to Nebraska the summer before senior year to work on an organic farm in the middle of nowhere. This is our punishment for that night—lazing away a beautiful summer day, floating on a lake with the sun warming our faces, our own little house and yard and what I am beginning to suspect will be minimal adult supervision. I thought my parents would at least put up something of a fight when I asked, but they gave in easily, as eager to get rid of me as your dad and wicked stepmother were to get rid of you. So here we are, but I am realizing that I am the only one who is punished.

I am the only one who actually sees you and the trouble that follows wherever you go. I don't have the luxury of passing you off to a different parent and buying you a plane ticket to another state. I'm the only one who knows. I'm the only one who ever knows. I'm the one who has to carry all of your secrets.

"Holy shit!" you say, and I feel you splash upright. "Look who lives right across from us."

I lift my head, and my feet brush against something suspicious in the water. I look across the lake and there he is—Dylan, sitting on the porch of the last cabin, directly across from our trailer. He has a book in one hand and a beer in the other. A shadow hides his eyes, but I can tell he is looking right at us.

"We need binoculars," you say.

I feel the lake boil.

A series of repeated actions: pulling and picking and setting down and turning over, left then right then up then down, over and over, one small movement after another until they add up to a conclusion—the compost is mixed in with that row of soil or these tomatoes are picked or this box is full of zucchini. We are the original conveyor belts, assembly lines, nothing but muscle and a few basic tools. This is what we've been doing since the beginning of civilization, taming the earth into something useful, making it do our bidding, our motions like prayer, like ritual. We massage the earth into an even greater fertility, and in return we ask for life.

There's only so much talking we can do until we run out of things to say. Then all there is in the way of entertainment is the feel of our bodies moving, the sun on our necks, the voices inside our heads. For a head case like me, this is heaven. The rhythm lulls my noisy brain into something manageable, focused, linear; what is usually swirling and amorphous is now sharp. The soil calms me. I hold it in my hands and feel my feet on the ground, solid, connected to something bigger and stronger than me.

But you act as if you are being tortured. Every minute that passes is a lifetime. Every time I look up, you are taking a break.

"I think I'm dehydrated," you say.

"But you already drank three water bottles."

"I'm so tired. My arms feel weak."

"It's because you're working. This isn't supposed to be easy."

"You don't have to be such a bitch."

You have always had a hard time staying in one place. There is nothing to do but be with yourself. The dirt does not distract you. These zucchini and tomatoes and greens and peppers do not distract you.

"Maybe I can get a job with the animals," you say.

"Maybe."

Three months of this to go. I wonder if you will ever stop complaining.

"Hey, look," you say. I follow your gaze into the distance, beyond the rows of kale and eggplant and something that looks like a green tomato bursting out of a paper lantern. And there is Dylan, mysterious and far away as usual.

"I wonder if we'll ever see him up close," you say. "It's like he's a ghost or something."

"I was thinking the same thing."

"What's that word I'm thinking of?"

"Enigma."

"Yeah." It no longer surprises us that I can read your mind. "Who's that with him?"

I squint. "I think it's Old Glen."

"Huh."

"I wonder where they're going."

Their clothes are clean, and they carry no tools. They don't look like they're planning on doing any hard labor.

"I want their job," you sigh. "Whatever it is."

I return to the zucchini, and you continue looking into the distance, as if you're searching for something to rescue you. The spiny fuzz of the vines is giving me a rash, but I don't mind. I'm strangely proud of it, like these red, itchy welts are battle wounds, some kind of mark for a rite of passage. Maybe the earth is claiming me as hers.

"Have you noticed that dirt smells a little bit like blood?" you say.

"Yes," I answer, and keep digging.

We peel off our sweaty, dirty clothes the second we get back to the trailer. You have your bikini on before I even have my pants off, and you're running into the lake as I'm still hopping into the leg holes of my swimsuit. I run in after you, feel the first shock of coolness, the sizzle through my veins, the relief like steam from my burning skin, then the embrace, my whole body submerged like yours, the ceasing of all sound, the weightlessness, the holding of breath. I open my eyes under the water and see hints of you, white flashes through the murky brown. I stay under for as long as I can bear it, and the pain of my lungs burning is almost exquisite, like it's something I've earned, like it's something you've given me.

The absence of air is what makes that first breath so delicious. The withholding, the starving, the torture—it's all for a purpose. We work all day for this, we endure pain for this: relief. This is something I've never been able to explain to you. We're opposites in this way like so many others. You are on the eternal quest for instant gratification, the now-now-now of stimulation, while I can wait for it forever, like the waiting is part of the pleasure, like I'm building a nest for it, making it a perfect home.

I wait until I can't stand it, and then I finally surface and breathe. It is a perfect breath.

"Look," you say.

He is there. Of course. Dylan. Across the lake, sitting in the late afternoon shadows under the eaves of his cabin. He leans back in his chair with his feet up on a milk crate, taking up as much space as possible, like you do. Even from this distance, I can tell that he is clean, like he hasn't lifted a finger all day.

"We're swimming over there, Max."

"What? Wait. No."

"Why not? We've got to meet him sometime."

"But we're wearing *swimsuits*."

"I know. It's perfect. Don't worry. You've got a hot bod."

Sometimes I think I could I hate you.

You part the lake with your body and pull me along in your wake. I panic for a moment when I realize we've reached the middle, that there's no turning back, that we're equidistant from the past and the future, and the only thing that makes any sense is going forward. There is no room for negotiation. We are at the deepest part of the lake and we don't know where the bottom is. It could go on forever, to the center of the earth, farther, strangled by water plants and all kinds of grabbing things. So we swim in the only direction left to us, and there is the shore, and there are his boots and his long legs in black jeans, and there is Dylan, watching us with a smirk on his lips.

The water spills off of you as you rise out of the water. You make it look effortless, as if you are being pulled up by some invisible force. You are shimmering, you are covered with diamonds, and I think this is what makes men believe in mermaids.

"Hello," you say in your liquid voice.

"Hi," he says, and his voice sounds exactly like I imagined it. Low and rough, like it is made out of gravel.

I follow you onto shore, but my feet stick in the mud, and I slip. I catch myself, but my legs and hands are covered with brown muck.

"Crap!"

"It's slippery there," he says.

"Yeah, I noticed."

"Are you okay?" you say. How is it possible that your feet aren't even muddy?

"I'm fine."

"What are you reading?" you ask him. He holds out the book. *Being and Nothingness*, by Jean-Paul Sartre. How much more hipster can someone get?

"Sar-tree," you say. "You read that for fun?"

"He's a smart guy."

"That's, like, philosophy, right?"

"Yeah, it's *like* philosophy," he says. There's something snakelike about him. Slithery.

"Max reads philosophy, don't you, Max?"

"A little."

"Oh yeah?" he says. "Like what?"

"Just the ancient Greeks and Romans, really. Like Socrates and Plato, Aristotle, Epicurus and Lucretius, Seneca. Stuff like that. Mostly just for historical context."

"Max speaks Latin," you say.

"No one *speaks* Latin," I mumble. I hate it when you do this, when you put me on display and show me off.

"Ask her anything about ancient Greece and I bet you she knows the answer," you say.

"Didn't they speak Greek in ancient Greece?" he says, leaning into his chair even farther, flicking a speck off his pants leg. I can't help but imagine that I am that speck.

I can't look him in the eye. "They don't offer ancient Greek as a language at our school."

"Yeah, that's generally not a class they have in high school." He is smiling, but it is not a nice smile.

Sadie seems completely unaware of Dylan's disdain. "Max is going to be a classics major. She's already, like, best friends with the head of the department at Oxford. That's in *England*. They're practically begging her to go there."

His smirk gets even smirkier. "Why would anyone want to study the classics?" He reaches over the side of his chair and lifts a silver flask from the floor of the porch. He takes a big swig, wipes his mouth with the back of his hand. "How irrelevant can you get?"

I am speechless. How am I supposed to answer quite possibly the rudest question I have ever been asked?

"Ooh, can I have some?" You reach out your hand, wiggling your fingers, too distracted by the shiny flask to even notice that your best friend was just supremely insulted.

He lifts his arm but doesn't move to hand it to you. "Come and get it," he says. You step forward and reach for the flask, slow and deliberate. You wrap your fingers around his before you pull it away. You have begun your mating dance. You drink too much, and your face reddens. I can tell you are trying not to cough. You are showing off for him.

"So, what do you do here?" you say.

"Things," he says.

"What kinds of things?"

"Various things."

"What were you and Old Glen doing today?"

"Stuff."

"You don't work in the fields?"

"Nope."

"You're lucky."

He doesn't say anything, just looks at us with disinterest.

"Do you ever get dirty?" you say. Oh God, Sadie. I am going to pretend you did not just say that.

"Sometimes," he says. He is looking at you with half-closed eyes.

"How old are you?" I say.

"Twenty-one."

"We're seventeen," I say.

"I know."

I can feel you burning next to me.

He stands up suddenly, stretching the full length of his body. His hands touch the ceiling of the porch, and for a second it looks like he's holding it up.

"If you'll excuse me, ladies, I have things to do."

"Okay," you say. "See you later." There is a tiny question in your voice, a crack in your confidence.

"Sure," he says without looking at us, then goes inside and shuts the door behind him.

You're bored. Of course you're bored. You get bored in Seattle, how could I expect a farm to entertain you? It's been four days, and already you're talking about stealing Doff's truck and driving until we find a city.

"Why don't we just ask him if we can borrow it?" I say.

"Fine." As if you hadn't even thought of this. You always want to do things the hard way.

Maybe I'm easily amused. Working, eating, swimming, reading, sleeping. That's all we're doing. In that order. Maybe it's enough for me. Maybe I'm made for a simple life tending the earth. Maybe my dreams of academic greatness and European adventures are a thing of the past, and instead of a world of history and myth and dusty old artifacts, all I really need is a plot of land to care for, the epic story reduced to the life and death of a vegetable, the trajectory of Western thought not much more than these trails of dirt in the creases of my palm.

"Do you know where you're going?" I say. I am always nervous when you drive.

"There's one road. We're going the direction Doff pointed. It's the only way *to* go."

The truck only has a radio, and it only picks up two stations: Country and Weird Jesus. We listen to Weird Jesus for a while because we think it'll be funny. But it's way more scary than funny, especially when the preacher starts talking about God being angry about homosexuals and Muslims and liberals and how he's going to punish everyone for their evil. He says nothing about how sad God must be that we all turned into such assholes.

We pass three trucks and two tractors. They all wave and smile, and I wonder if they're listening to the same radio station, wonder if they believe what the preacher says, wonder how they can be so friendly if they're filled with so much hate.

It takes half an hour to get to the "town" of Hazeldon. We know we're there because a sign tells us so. WELCOME TO HAZELDON. POPULATION: 873. You squeal when we have to stop at a stop sign. "Civilization!" you cry.

But when we look around, all we see are a couple of rickety houses and a brown horse scratching its rump on a tree. An unattended roadside stand with ears of corn lined up on a table, a shoebox with a slot in the top that says "5 for $1." Some kind of vulture flies in circles overhead.

"The town," you say. "Where is it?"

"It's got to be somewhere."

You dodge a dozen or so cows wandering the road. They moo at us as we drive by, as if annoyed at our intrusion. The Weird Jesus preacher is yelling at us, telling us to *Repent!* I can hear the spit hissing out of his mouth.

"Yes!" you proclaim, and I think for a second you've found the Lord, but then I see what you're staring at ahead of us. Buildings. None of them over one story, but buildings nonetheless. Not many, but enough to warrant a few blocks of sidewalk and a couple more stop signs. There are parked cars and a scattering of people walking. As we get closer, we can read a sign advertising Millie's Diner, Big Ben's Hardware & Feed, the Hazeldon Post Office, a grocery store, a Quick Stop gas station, a white Catholic church and a baby-blue Lutheran church, like all the little pieces of a toy set of a town.

You're looking around frantically, like you're afraid you missed something, like maybe there's a club hiding between these little quaint buildings, maybe one of your favorite bands is playing tonight amid the corn. But all we see are a couple of old men in cowboys hats, sitting outside the coffee shop smoking cigarettes, a middle-aged woman with a tragic haircut, carrying grocery bags to her dented minivan, an old lady making her slow way up the Catholic church steps. The people are all shaped like those Little People toys, kind of like roundish squares.

You pull into a space in front of the diner. I can see your jaw grinding, your lips thin.

"Want a milkshake?" I say.

"Fine."

The old men nod at us as we pass. They appear to be made out of leather. The inside of the café is all vinyl booths and checkerboard linoleum. It smells like decades' worth of grease, cigarette smoke, disinfectant, and burnt coffee, and the stained floral wallpaper seems to have been hanging there the whole time. The place is empty.

"Hello?" I say because you don't. You are standing with your arms crossed in front of your chest, your sunglasses still hiding your eyes.

"Sit anywhere you like," a voice yells from somewhere through the window to the kitchen.

We take a booth near the window. You stare at the backs of the old men's heads as I open the plastic-covered menu on the table.

"Ooh, fries!" I say. You don't respond, just keep looking out the window.

A woman in an apron approaches. She could be anywhere from her midthirties to her fifties.

"You girls from Oasis?" she asks, neither friendly nor unfriendly.

"Yes," I say. "Is it that obvious?"

She half smiles. "Pretty much."

I order us a chocolate milkshake and fries to share. As soon as the waitress leaves, you take off your sunglasses and look me in the eyes. "Max, I don't think I'm going to make it."

"Don't be so dramatic."

"No, seriously. I feel like screaming every five minutes."

"Then scream. I'm sure no one would mind. You can tell them it's some kind of therapy."

"I'm serious, Max. I can't do a whole summer of this. I just can't."

I can hear the sizzle of the French fries cooking and the whirr of the milkshake machine. You've got tears in your eyes and a look on your face like the world is ending.

"But you were so excited, remember?" I say. "To get out of Seattle and spend the summer with your mom finally."

A long, wet tear streaks down your cheek and makes a puddle on the table. "But I've barely even seen her," you choke out. "It's like she doesn't even want me here." The tears keep coming, and the puddle gets bigger. It will drown us if I don't manage to cheer you up.

"She's busy, Sadie. Everyone is. Remember how she said there's a lot to do right now but there's a break between harvests soon? And everyone will have more time and energy to do other stuff?"

"Uh huh." You wipe your wet nose with the back of your hand. The waitress delivers our order, setting two milkshakes on the table.

"I made a little extra," she says. "On the house. Looked like you needed it."

I am speechless for a moment, but I finally manage to say, "Thank you." Your face becomes a waterfall and you blubber an earnest "You are so *nice*." The waitress smiles and shrugs as if her kindness is unremarkable, as if people do things like that all the time. She says, "Enjoy, girls," and I want to hug her.

"See," I tell you. "Things are looking up."

You nod and sniffle.

"It's just culture shock," I say. "You'll get used to it. We're going to have fun, I promise."

You take a long sip of the milkshake and close your eyes. I'm afraid you're going to start crying again, but then you say,

"Oh my God, this is *so fucking good*." I taste it. You are right. It is the best milkshake I have ever tasted in my life.

"What do they put in these things?" you say.

"Crack," I say. "It must be crack."

We each grab a fry and dunk it in our milkshakes. Some people have not experienced the great delicacy that is French fries dipped in chocolate milkshake. Their lives are incomplete.

"Oh my God."

"Jesus Christ."

"Hallelujah."

For a few minutes, everything feels just right. Your cheeks dry as we fill ourselves with grease and fat and sugar. This is the Sadie I love, the girl who smiles with a little of my help. And you do, the fries and milky shake squishing out of your teeth like a rabies froth.

"Do you like seafood?" you say.

"You're so dumb, Sadie," I say, but the air is light.

"See food!" You open your mouth wide to give me a good view of its squishy contents. I throw a fry at your face, and you catch it with your teeth. "Ta da!"

But then everything shifts. The air is hot and oppressive once again. You have the power to do this with just the darting of your eyes to the opening door. Your ears perk at the sound of the bells ringing, and I watch our new visitor as he approaches the counter.

You lean over and whisper, "I love me some farm boy." I can smell the greasy sweetness of your breath.

"Shhh," I say. "Gross." Your eyes have that twinkle that usually means trouble.

"Max, look at his ass! These guys have actual *muscles*."

I can't help it. I look. His ass is indeed miraculous. You don't find asses like that on the skinny wannabe hipsters in Seattle, whose greatest athletic achievement is carrying a guitar case.

"Hey, Mom!" he calls into the kitchen. He sits on a stool and spins around, stopping midspin when he sees us.

"Hi," you say, twisting your straw between your fingertips.

"Hi," he says with a surprisingly shy smile. He's not that cute according to our usual criteria. He is definitely no Dylan, not one of the bad boys you usually go for. But I guess he has an all-American charm, with his short, sandy blond hair and freckles.

"I'm Sadie and this is Max. We're here for the summer."

"I'm Seth. You staying at Oasis?"

"Why does everyone assume that?" you flirt.

"Um," he says, not catching the teasing. "Because you're new? And no one new ever comes here except to work at Oasis?"

"Oh," you say. You do that giggle I hate, the one that makes you sound like a bimbo.

Seth spins back to face the counter as his mom comes out of the kitchen. She ruffles his hair and says, "Hi, sweetie," and his eyes dart in our direction as his face reddens.

"Mom," he says softly.

"He doesn't want us to hear him," you whisper devilishly, hopefully not loud enough for them to hear.

"Can I have twenty dollars?" he says.

"What for? I just gave you ten yesterday."

"He wants to buy us flowers," you say, a little too loudly. "And champagne."

"Sadie, *shhh*," I whisper.

"I just need to get some groceries."

"It's pretty cheap champagne," you say.

"I just bought groceries," the waitress says.

"But we're worth it," you say.

"But you didn't get any of the stuff I like," Seth whines. I take it back—there's actually nothing attractive about him.

"What, like junk?" the waitress says, but pulls a few bills out of her apron anyway, hands him one. "Ten dollars. That's it." She ruffles his hair again and walks back into the kitchen.

"Thanks, Mom," he calls after her.

"A rare glimpse of the rural teen in his natural environment," you say. "Fascinating stuff."

"Fascinating," I fake-agree.

"Hey, Seth!" you shout across the empty restaurant.

He turns around to face us, his face turning red once again.

"Tell us about the nightlife in Hazeldon," you say, patting the booth. He blinks and cocks his head like a confused puppy. "Have a seat," you say, and he comes as instructed.

Seth takes a seat next to you and doesn't seem to know where to put his hands. "Um, there's not really any *nightlife* here." He says "nightlife" like it's a foreign word, like he doesn't quite know how to pronounce it.

"What do you do for fun?" Sadie says. "Like what are you doing tonight? Like right now? What are you *really* going to spend that ten dollars on?"

"Um, chips?" he says. "And pop?" He seems acutely aware that he is giving you the wrong answer.

You sigh. "Let's try again, Seth. What are you and your friends doing tonight?"

"Well, I'm babysitting my sister tonight," he says. "Probably playing video games after she goes to sleep. Before that, she usually makes me watch a stupid princess movie.'

You slump over the table and hold your head in your hands, slowly shaking it back and forth in exasperation. "Seth, you gotta work with me here." Poor Seth.

"Wait!" he says, his face lighting up. You're skeptical. "There's a party tomorrow night! A big one. Everyone's going." He has your full attention now. "At the abandoned barn out on Fuller Road. Do you know where that is?"

"As a matter of fact, I do not," you say, grinning. "Would you like to tell me?"

"Yeah," Seth says. "You should come. It'll be real fun."

"We'd be delighted. Wouldn't we, Max?"

"Delighted," I agree. I suddenly feel very tired.

Seth draws directions on a napkin, then leaves for his exciting night of chip eating and pop drinking and princess movie watching. You hold up the napkin proudly, like it's some valuable artifact in your anthropological study of the farm boy. "Max, we're going to a party."

"Yippee," I say, mock-enthusiastically.

Seth's mom gives us the check and takes our plate and glasses. "You girls running out of things to do?" she says, not nearly as friendly as she was before.

"A little bit," you say.

"Well, don't go looking too hard," she says, then walks away.

You look at me and mouth *What's her problem?* I say nothing about how I imagine a mother would feel about her son inviting you to a party.

You're a lot more useful when you're excited about something. The party is tonight, and you actually did some work today instead of taking breaks every ten minutes to combat imaginary heat stroke.

You stay at the trailer to take a "beauty nap" while I walk up to the main house. We've been here almost a week now, and I figure it's time to finally call my parents. I left a message on Monday, but I called when I knew my dad was at work and wouldn't be there to pick up the phone. Mom was home, but I knew she wouldn't answer either.

There are a few people puttering around in the kitchen, taking showers, and lounging on the patio. Skyler is painting a hideous watercolor of the lake, wearing a stupid pink beret on her head even though it's a million degrees outside. She takes a break to glare at me.

"Where's Sadie?" she asks.

"Taking a nap."

"What are you doing here?"

"Making a phone call."

"Long distance?"

"Yes," I say, not that it's any of her business.

"You have to pay us back, you know," Skyler says with her nose in the air. "We're not just going to pay for your phone calls."

"I know," I say. Skyler rolls her eyes, and I make my way into the living room.

Dylan is sitting in the corner by the ancient computer with his feet up on the back of a couch. He watches me enter the room like I'm some bug crawling across the floor he's too lazy to step on. He turns his body to the wall and talks low into the phone so I can't make out anything he's saying.

I try to act cool, but I'm not sure how I'm supposed to behave, alone in a room with someone scary and beautiful who's having a conversation on the phone he doesn't want me to hear. I pretend like I'm perusing the bookshelves—years' worth of old *National Geographic*s; books about organic gardening, animal husbandry, herbal medicine, and self-sufficiency; some old paperback novels; biographies; books of poetry; miscellaneous textbooks. I pull out a *National Geographic* from the nineties and lie down on a couch, trying to look as relaxed as possible, like I don't even know Dylan's there whispering secrets in the corner, like it's totally normal for me to be in a weird room with a weird guy and not feel weird. The text of the magazine is too small and too long to read, so I flip through the pages just looking at the pictures. I look at a picture of a buffalo standing knee-deep in a mud puddle and think I hear Dylan mumble "big" or "pig," or maybe "wig." At a picture of a flock of pink flamingos, I hear him say "clear" or "here," possibly "queer." At something that looks like a miniature deer, he says "yeah." Hippo, "no." Cheetah, "fuck." Hyena, "hell, no." He is not mumbling anymore. His voice is loud and clear. Lion, "A deal's a deal, man." Big lion, "That's fucking right." Big angry lion, "Fuck you." Big angry lion attacking a warthog, "All right then." Dead, mangled, bloody body of a warthog, "All right." Pause, quiet, text on a page. Advertisement for American Express with a photo of a sunset over the Grand Canyon, "Yeah, bye."

"What are you looking at?"

"Huh?" I say.

He's looking straight at me with a scowl on his face.

"I need to use the phone," I say.

"So use it." He gets up and walks out of the room, taking

the air with him. I feel my stomach drop. I want to run after him, want to scream *No, wait!* want to explain that I was not eavesdropping, that I am not the loser he thinks I am, that I am not just some dumb kid. But he's gone, and I'm left with the phone like a torture device.

It is early afternoon in Seattle and I know my dad is home. He never goes anywhere on the weekends. He hasn't figured out a way to escape besides work. He will answer the phone, and I will have to talk to him.

Sadie, why do you have to be sleeping? Why can't you be here sitting next to me while I do this?

He picks up on the third ring. "Hello?" he says, and I can tell from that tiny word that he is so tired.

"Hi, Dad."

"Maxie!" he says. "Oh, it's so good to hear from you. Sorry we missed your call the other day. How are things there?"

"Okay."

"Having fun?"

"Yeah, I guess."

"How's Sadie?"

"Good."

"Is the work hard?"

"Kind of. Not too bad. I'm getting strong."

"A little physical labor is good for everyone."

"Yeah."

Pause. Silence. There is nothing else we are allowed to talk about.

"How are you?" I venture.

"Oh, good, everything's good. Work is busy. Mariners are doing awful this season. You know, the usual."

"How's mom?"

Intake of breath, hold. Remember how to say something while saying nothing.

"Oh, well, she's tired, you know."

"Is she there?"

"Yeah, well, honey, I think she's sleeping right now."

"Can you check?"

"No, I'm pretty sure she's sleeping."

"Oh."

"Sorry, sweetie—maybe next time, okay?"

"Okay."

"Alright then."

"I have to go get ready for a party," I say.

"A party! That's great!"

"Yeah."

"It's great to hear you two are making friends!"

"Yeah."

"Just great!"

I know things are bad when he starts talking with exclamation points.

"Bye, Dad."

"Bye, honey. Say hi to Sadie."

"Say hi to Mom."

"Love you, kiddo."

"Love you too."

Hang up. Dial tone. An empty room full of dust. It floats around like the ghosts of sad fairies, catching the light only to show how dead it is.

You're driving to the party, but we both know I'll be the one driving us back.

Usually we wait to arrive at a party extra fashionably late so you can make your grand appearance and convince people you have tons of other places to be. But you couldn't wait this time, and we're on our way even though it isn't even dark yet. The Weird Jesus station is on full blast, and the preacher is screaming so loud I can feel it in my bones, and you're screaming right along with him, shouting "Amen!" and "Hallelujah!" out the window at the cows. I have no idea what he's talking about, and I know you don't either, but he says it with such passion and conviction I can see how someone might be scared not to believe him.

I didn't tell you about the phone call with my dad. I know when it's not a good time to bother you with my problems.

We follow the napkin directions past town into an identical expanse of corn and cows. The sun starts to set and everything glistens golden, including you. The angle of the light makes your cheekbones even sharper, your lips even fuller, your neck even longer, and I have that feeling I get sometimes when I read something so beautiful I have to close my eyes and take a deep breath, then read it again.

And then there it is: a big red barn in the middle of a field with a scattering of cars, mostly trucks, parked in the flattened grass around it. I turn down Weird Jesus, and the thin, tinny sound of electric guitars fills the air; whatever music they're listening to has no bass. A few people circle a bonfire, red plastic cups or beer cans in their hands. If I squint my eyes just right, this could be any party, anywhere.

"Holy shit, is that a mullet?" you say as you park the truck. "A real live non-ironic mullet?"

It could be a mullet. It could also just be a normal haircut you want to believe is a mullet. To be honest, the people here don't look all that different from people in Seattle. The only difference seems to be that they're not trying as hard, they're not as desperate to define themselves by their clothing.

"There's Seth," you say, waving. He walks over, his face

immediately turning a deep shade of red. A few people look at us curiously.

"Thanks for coming," he says.

"Our pleasure," you say. "Now, where can I get a drink?"

You drink. And you drink. At first there's only beer, and I feel momentary relief, but then older people arrive with bottles of liquor, and I switch into super-vigilant take-care-of-Sadie mode. It doesn't take long for you to turn the whole party into your audience, all the boys in rapt attention, all the girls huddled around the bonfire silently plotting your demise. You brag about Seattle, and you keep calling it "the City," like it's New York or San Francisco, even though no one ever calls it the City. You keep telling everyone how you live only minutes away from the house where Kurt Cobain killed himself, and they all *ooh* and *aah* as expected.

It is just like any other night from our old lives, but instead of wannabe indie rockers, we're hanging out with high school football players and ex–high school football players, and instead of smoking weed in the park, we're drinking cheap beer next to an old barn. Instead of city lights, there are stars all around us. The music of the fields mixes with the drawls of the boys' voices and smooths out your sharp edges just a little. But I'm still sitting here quietly, watching you flirt with boys I know you don't even like. You're still putting on a show, wrapping these strangers around your finger. I don't know what I was expecting, but I guess I was hoping that a summer away from our lives would somehow be a summer away from this. I did not figure that no matter where we go, we take ourselves with us.

Once again, I am watching the Sadie Show. This is a special episode, on location in the middle of Nebraska with a whole new set of extras, except the plotline is identical to all the other episodes. You get drunk, I stay sober; you do your little song and dance, I stand by ready to catch you if you trip; you disappear, I freak out; you reappear with messy hair and slurred speech and proceed to say inappropriate things. This is when it's my turn to shine, whisking you away before you get into too much trouble, a thankless job half of the time because you won't even remember.

It is barely dark before you run off into the corn with some guy with long greasy hair, a tattoo of a shotgun on his forearm, and a bottle of rum. I do my best to make small talk with the people at the party, telling them over and over again where I'm from and what I'm doing here. I keep looking at the wall of corn where you disappeared, illuminated by the twirling light of the bonfire, shadows like an experimental movie projection at one of those weird "noise" shows you pretend to enjoy.

Finally you emerge, glassy-eyed and grinning, your hair

tangled with weeds. The greasy guy follows, slithering off into a huddle of boys in the shadows. You seem to have forgotten him completely as you run into my arms.

"Max!" you say. "This is a fun party, right?"

"It's okay."

"I need to sit down."

Most of the party is gathered around the bonfire, so that is where I take you. I figure you'll be safer in the light, where I can share the task of watching you with others. I try to prop you up on a milk crate, but you have a better idea. "Hay bales!" you exclaim. "I want to sit on a hay bale!"

A girl wearing way too much makeup rolls her eyes as she scoots over to make room, and my heart drops into my stomach. You did not see her, did not see the judgment and disgust in her eyes. But I did. So I feel it for you, feel the embarrassment and shame you would be feeling if you were conscious. People are looking at us and whispering; even the fire seems to be laughing. You are laughing too, but you don't know that you are the joke.

"Max," you say, leaning into me. Your lips are wet with spit. "These are like the people in that movie *Boys Don't Cry*."

"No, they're not."

"Yes, they are! They're going to kill that girl with the big teeth."

"Sadie, shut up."

"What's her name?"

"Hilary Swank."

"Oh my God, they're going to kill Hilary Swank!" Heads turn, and you are oblivious.

"Sorry," I say to the crowd. "Sadie, I think it's time to go," I say to you.

"Max, they think you're going to hell."

"Seriously, let's go."

"I can't believe they think that."

"Sadie."

"How could they? Don't they know how nice you are? Don't they know you're the best person in the whole world?" You are getting worked up. You are yelling at the bonfire.

"Someone shut that girl up," a shrill voice says, and my heart shatters in my chest, sends shrapnel cutting through my ribs.

You are trying to stand up. You raise your arm in the air as if declaring war. I try to pull you down, but you can be so strong when you want to be. "Why do you think my Max is going to hell? What is wrong with you people?"

A few people away, Seth laughs, still charmed by you, still playing along. "Why are you going to hell, Max?"

"Because she's *bisexual*, you rednecks," you announce to the entire state of Nebraska. "She fucks chicks!"

Oh. My. God.

Shocked silence and a few nervous giggles. I am stone. I can only see the ground, dead grass, bottle cap, cigarette butts, crumpled-up piece of paper, my feet in sandals, chipped orange nail polish, one blond hair on my right big toe.

I hate you, Sadie. I hate you so much.

Then someone says, "So what?"

I look up, look around at all the faces, expecting to see the burning hatred in their eyes, but no one's even looking at me. Most have returned to previous conversations, some are still eyeing Sadie with annoyance, but no one's even looking at me. No one's going to gay bash me. No one's going to call me a sinner. No one's even going to show the customary straight-guy interest in the bisexual threesome fantasy. And I don't know which is worse—being hated or being ignored—but here we are, the two of us, unwelcome in our opposite ways.

"Let's go, Sadie," I say quietly.

"Okay," you agree, because despite how drunk you are, I know you can tell that they've already decided we're gone.

I help you walk to the truck, and no one says goodbye, not even Seth.

You pass out as soon as I pull onto the road. The silence is a relief. Your head is on my lap and you are curled up on the seat in the fetal position. This is when you are most beautiful—when you are still, when you have let go, when you are mine to take care of. But somehow it feels different tonight, in this place that is so different from our usual haunts, with these people who have not been trained to love you. Somehow it doesn't seem like such an honor to be your best friend, your other half, the one who completes you. I suddenly feel so exhausted, so tired of this job I've had for so many years. So tired of your messes. So tired of always being the one to clean them up.

But you reach out your arm and wrap it around my stomach. You burrow your face into my leg. I feel your warmth through my bones, and my anger melts away, leaving only a trail of sadness, a feeling so less sturdy.

We have been in this position so many times, with me as the chauffeur of your regret, both of us silent on the ride home from an event we will never talk about. But I remember. I always remember. One of us has to.

I pull up to the house and park the truck. I help you out even though you insist on staying. "I can sleep in here," you mumble. "It's soft. It has doors." I do most of the walking as I drag you to the path that leads to our trailer. Your face is pressed against mine. You smell awful.

The night is so still that when I hear the murmur of voices across the lake it sounds amplified. The stars are bright enough that I can make out two figures in the darkness. They are coming out of the half-finished yurt near Dylan's at the end of the row, the one no one lives in. I stop and squint my eyes, adjust my arm around you so you don't fall. One of the figures is Marshall. His giant body and shoulder-length curls make it obvious. The other figure is smaller, a woman. Marshall leans over and kisses her. She is wrapped in a sheet, her shoulders bare. It is not his wife. Not Skyler's mother.

It is yours. It is Lark in Marshall's arms.

Sadie, tonight is full of so much heartbreak, and you don't even know it. And I will not tell you. It is my job to hold it for both of us.

Something is very wrong.

Even after your worst binges, your hangovers never last this long. It's been four days since the party, and it just seems to be getting worse. I'm used to you complaining that you're tired, but this time it doesn't seem like an act. You can barely get a shovel to break the earth. Yesterday you fainted while picking tomatoes.

"My throat hurts," you croak as we walk to breakfast. We're late. Some people have already finished eating and are heading out to the fields. It took me forever to get you out of bed this morning, and I'm trying to hurry you to the house, but you refuse to go much faster than a slug. "Feel my forehead," you say. I am losing my patience. I am starving.

"Fine." I put my back of my hand on your forehead. You are burning up. "Shit," I say.

"It's hot, huh?"

I nod. I don't know what to do. This is something I can't fix.

"I can't work today," you say. "I'm sorry."

We stand there for a moment, in the middle of the trail, not talking. Are you asking for my permission? Are you waiting for me to say it's okay for you to go back to bed?

"You should get some rest," I finally say, and it feels a little like defeat, like you won this round. Sadie: 1; Max: 0. "I'll find Lark and tell her you're sick."

"Thank you." You seem relieved with your victory. "I'm sorry, Max."

"I know."

I know it's not your fault that you're sick, but I can't help being a little mad at you. It's always something, isn't it? Something to make you a little less accountable, something to force me to take up the slack.

I find Lark cleaning up in the kitchen. I see a flash of her and Marshall from the other night, her naked shoulders painted with moonlight, her hair wild with the aftermath of sex, and I get a sick feeling in my stomach. But it passes, and I just see you there in the dark. Anger is replaced by a kind of apathetic sadness, a halfhearted disappointment. Of course Lark is cheating on Doff. She's your mother, isn't she?

"Darling!" she says when she sees me. "Where's your other half?"

"She's sick. Really sick. Like I think she needs to go to the doctor."

Her face falls, but not like a mother's who is worried about her daughter. "The nearest clinic is almost an hour away," she finally says. She is annoyed. This is an inconvenience for her. "It's probably the flu," she says, a hint of guilt showing in her eyes.

"But her throat hurts too. She says it's swollen. It could be something worse. She might need antibiotics or something."

I can tell Lark doesn't know what to say, and I suddenly get it. I understand how a mother could abandon her child and run off to have her own adventures. Maybe Lark doesn't have the gene or whatever it is that makes you want to take care of someone else, to think of someone else's feelings at all.

Her usual carefree confidence dims. She is unsure of herself in this unfamiliar territory. I must take the lead. "Call the clinic," I tell her. "Tell them we're coming. I'll get Sadie." Lark nods, and she looks like you when you've done something wrong.

When I get back to the trailer, I find you shivering. You

have pulled all the blankets off both of our beds and are wrapped in a cocoon in the corner, with just the fuzzy pink top of your head sticking out. "I'm freezing," you say, but it's already at least eighty degrees outside. When I pull the blankets down, your face is drenched with sweat. "Everything hurts," you moan, and you start to cry.

I manage to get you dressed. You insist on wearing as many layers as possible and bringing the blankets with us. Your skin is hot and slippery with sweat, but you're shaking like you're naked in the snow.

It takes a while, but we make it to the house where Lark is waiting. "Mommy!" you cry and shove yourself at her. She doesn't quite know what to do with the giant crying ball of blankets, but she puts her arms around you as best she can.

"The clinic's expecting you," she says to me.

You pull the blankets off your head. "You're coming, aren't you?" You stare at your mother with a child's heartbreak, and the beginnings of tears push the fever from your eyes. Lark's eyes go wide with fear and shock. She had no idea she was supposed to even consider such a thing.

"Oh, um, yes, of course," she says. "Of course I'm coming with you." She glances at me for a split second, as if checking to make sure she got away with the lie.

I drive. You lie across us with your head on Lark's lap. She runs her fingers through your hair but says nothing. It is a long, silent drive. I don't feel like listening to the radio, don't want to hear sad twangy songs or someone yelling at me about my sins. At one point, you burst awake and shove the blankets off you almost violently, tearing off your layers of clothes until you're wearing only a tank top and underwear. "Open all the windows!" you cry. "I'm melting!" You hang your head out the window the rest of the way there, panting like a dog.

The clinic is just past Hazeldon, not much more than a little house with a sign. Lark and I wait in the tiny lobby on plastic chairs while you go with the doctor. A middle-aged woman sits across from us reading a *People* magazine from two years ago. She looks up when we sit down, purses her lips, and goes back to her magazine.

"You're a good friend, Max," Lark says.

"Thanks."

"What do you think is wrong with her?"

"I don't know. I'm not a doctor." I realize that must have sounded bitchy, but I don't really care. Lark is quiet for a minute. I pretend to look at a wrinkled edition of *Crafting Quarterly* magazine. I still haven't eaten.

"I'm going to find a store and get something to eat," I say, standing up. "Want anything?"

"No, thank you."

I move toward the door, but Lark grabs my hand. "Wait," she says. "Sit for a minute."

"I'm starving."

"Here," she says, pulling a granola bar out of her Indian-print fabric purse. "See, I'm not totally useless." She tries to laugh, but that just makes what she said even sadder.

We sit there in silence while I eat the granola bar. The woman across from us keeps sighing loudly, like she wants us to hear her, like she is trying to tell us something.

"Is Sadie okay?" Lark says, not looking up from her knees.

"I don't know. We have to wait to see what the doctor says."

"No, I mean in general. In Seattle. Is she okay?"

I don't say anything for a while. I try to think of how to package my answer, how to best protect you. But then I realize that the granola bar didn't make me feel better at all, it just made me hungrier, and I'm so tired and so frustrated and so sick of always thinking of you first.

"No," I say. "She's not okay."

Lark is quiet for a moment, then says, "I got that impression."

I feel anger welling up inside of me. I want to say, *What, do you want a trophy? Should I congratulate you for noticing that your kid's fucked up?*

"She seems lost," Lark says.

I want to say, *Well, what do you fucking expect?* But instead I just say, "Yes."

"What is it like? What is her life like in Seattle?"

I stare at Lark, hard, until she finally looks up from her knees. She looks at me with such sadness, such regret, that my heart loosens a little. Your pain isn't entirely her fault. Few things are ever entirely one person's fault. She looks at me with yearning, with a real desire to understand. Sadie, it's not just you who is lost. It's not just you stuck in the middle of nowhere.

"She needs a mother," I finally say.

Lark buries her face in her hands. Her body shudders as she weeps. I put my hand on her back and rub in slow circles the way I remember my mother doing when I was a kid and needed to cry. The lady sitting across from us looks up and grimaces, her face contorted in judgment. "What?" I say too loudly. She gets up in a huff and moves to a chair on the other end of the waiting area.

I don't want to talk anymore. I want to be in the field with the sun on my back and the dirt in my hands. I want to feel my muscles burn at the end of the day, want the pure satisfaction of physical labor, my body telling me I've done enough, I can rest, I've earned it, I'm allowed to let everything go. I let

Lark cry. I let the grumpy woman sit in the corner and judge us. I try to imagine what it would feel like to not care how they feel.

The doctor enters the waiting room and tells us to come with him. He leads us down a short hallway into an exam room, where you are sitting on the examination table, your bare feet dangling off the side, a Styrofoam cup of water in your hand. You are pale, but you smile when we enter. "Have a seat," the doctor says, and Lark takes the chair closest to you, holding your hand in hers.

"We won't know for sure until the tests come back in a couple days," the doctor begins. "But I'm pretty certain Sadie has mono. She has a lot of flulike symptoms, her temp's a hundred and two, but her lymph nodes are definitely swollen and her spleen is slightly enlarged. Those things usually don't happen with just a flu."

"Is that bad?" Lark asks.

"Well, she'll get better, but it'll take some time. Mono's a virus, so no antibiotics are going to help. Unless she gets strep, too, which is highly likely. For now, she just needs a lot of rest. And ibuprofen for the fever. Drink lots of water and eat well. Popsicles are great for the sore throat. Gargle with salt water."

"How long is 'some time'?" I ask.

"She'll probably start feeling better in three or four weeks, but she'll need to take it easy for a couple months. Especially no strenuous physical activity, because of the enlarged spleen. It can rupture really easily if she's not careful, which would be a real nightmare."

"So no work at all?" I say, surprised at my own voice. "We work on a farm. That's, like, what we *do*."

"Unfortunately, no," the doctor says. "She should really stay in bed until she starts feeling better. Another thing is that this is highly contagious. I understand that you live in a very close-knit community and share the same facilities and utensils with several people?" He looks at his clipboard as he says this, as if he doesn't want to dignify the statement with eye contact.

"Yes," Lark says.

"I'm sorry to tell you this, but it might be a good idea to quarantine her for a while. At least until she stops coughing for a few days in a row. Make sure she doesn't share plates or cups or silverware with anyone."

"Quarantine?" you say. "Like, be *alone*?" This is your worst nightmare.

"You don't want to get all your, um, your . . . *people* sick, do you?"

"No," you whimper.

"They might already be infected, actually. It's pretty

hard to avoid when you're living so closely with such a large group."

"Oh no," you cry. "What if I got everyone sick?"

"Nobody's sick, Sadie," I say, glaring at the doctor. "Don't worry, everything's going to be fine."

Lark is by your side as we leave the room. She crosses her fingers as the receptionist runs her credit card. She sighs with relief when the card is approved. You sleep the whole way back, curled into the fetal position, trying to turn yourself into a baby, trying to go back in time. Lark stares out the window, her eyes distant and wet.

I can't help but be reminded of a similar drive we took long before, in what now seems like another world, with me in the driver's seat as usual and you curled up beside me, trying to make yourself as small as possible. But instead of sun and golden fields and blue sky, it was winter in Seattle. The road was a swamp of brown slush, and everything else was the gray and white of thick clouds and old snow. Everything around us, cold and lifeless. And you, groggy and fragile beside me, and for the first time in our lives, I could not imagine what you were feeling.

This was two years ago, the winter of sophomore year. There was no question it would be me who would take you. You never had to say I'd be the only one who would ever know. Not even the father, although you refused to call him that. You preferred "That Guy" or "Sperm Donor." You refused to even call him by name. And as much as I tried to get you to talk about it, all you could do was pretend you had no feelings at all, like it was just as routine a medical procedure as getting your wisdom teeth out. You joked, "Oh, come on, Max, you're not getting all pro-life on me, are you? Next you're going to tell me you signed up for one of those camps where they pray the gay out of you."

But the sound coming out of your mouth was not laughter. I could tell beneath it you were choking, you were gasping for air, you were screaming for someone to hold you. I tried, but you wouldn't let me. You pushed me away and said I was being melodramatic.

"Just because you call yourself a feminist doesn't mean this isn't a big deal," I said.

"This is only a big deal if I make it a big deal," was your response. "I don't want it to be a big deal. Therefore, it is not. It's simple logic."

But it was not, Sadie. It is never that simple with you.

You were so quiet on that car ride home. "Are you in pain?" I asked.

"They gave me good drugs." Your voice sounded like it does when you're drunk. After a minute, you said, "The snow is pretty. I like it when it covers everything, before it starts to melt. When it makes everything go away."

I thought you fell asleep, but then I saw the slightest movement. You placed a hand on your belly, and suddenly your fingers seemed so thin and frail. You think your big sunglasses hide everything, but I saw the tears running past the rims and collecting on your chin, making a wet stalactite of sorrow. I saw your chin tremble as you held your breath. I saw you mouth the words, *I'm sorry*.

This, too, this sickness now—it is something some boy gave you. You will inevitably blame him, whoever he was. His mouth on yours. The invisible virus. Mono is not called "the Kissing Disease" for nothing. Sadie, there is so much pain passed between bodies. And you have felt it all.

ᾌδης
HADES

There is always water on the way to the under-world, rivers with heavy names like Sorrow, Hate, and Lamentation. Even here, there is currency, an underground economy of coins placed in silent mouths, payment for safe passage across sad waters made of tears.

What do the dead say with money on their tongues? Are their words worth more than empty ones?

This is where you go when there's nothing left for you in the sun, when your body has lost its value and all that's left is your tiny speck of a soul, not nearly as valuable as you always thought it was. Not divine, not profound—just a small, flimsy thing to be piled in a cave and hoarded by a lonely god.

He had a family once. Maybe he wasn't always so lonely.

But, like so many of us, he lost a bet and his fate was sealed. For eternity, he will hold on to his dead, obsess over his macabre collection. It will tower around him—these souls, these coins—but he will always be lonely, buried in this darkness no one ever willingly visits.

Even the god of darkness can be afraid of the dark.

When we get back, you go straight to bed. You sleep through my packing, adding your own soundtrack of wheezy, poisonous breaths. Lark brings a wheelbarrow, and we carry all my stuff around the lake. You get to keep the trailer, and I'm stuck in the half-built yurt at the end of the trail where, until now, your mother was carrying on her affair with Marshall.

When we get there, I can't help but look for signs. I feel a sick compulsion to find something, anything—messed-up sheets, stray hairs, a condom wrapper. But it's spotless. They removed all evidence they were ever here. There's just a folded cot against the wall, a rickety dresser, a little table and chair, some hooks on the wall. The only sign of life is a small crystal hanging in front of the window, spreading rainbow polka dots of afternoon sun through the room like a disco ball.

"It's not as nice as the trailer, I know," Lark says. "But better this than getting what Sadie has, right?" I nod. "I'll go get you some sheets and blankets and a lantern. The cot's really comfy, actually." She doesn't mention how she knows that.

Lark leaves me to my new house, and I put my clothes away in the dresser, set up the cot by the window, wipe it down with a wet cloth, doing everything I can to push the thought of bodily fluids from my mind. The two small windows have thin screens stapled across them, with no glass or shutters or curtains. The walls are an octagon of naked beams and particleboard. There is no electricity. The canvas roof is missing, with only rafters and tarps keeping the elements out. A porch hasn't been built yet, and there's just a wobbly crate as a step. The only shade is inside the yurt, but it's so stuffy it's no relief. This is a skeleton of a home.

I look across the lake at what used to my home with you. It is so strange to see it from this perspective, surreal almost, like I am living in a mirror. I look to the right and see Dylan's small cabin, with nothing outside but a chair on the porch and some empty beer bottles. Everyone is gone, out in the fields or doing other chores. It feels like a ghost town. And I am the ghost.

I sit in the doorway with my feet on the crate, trying not to feel sorry for myself. But I don't know what else to feel. I suddenly feel so lonely, like whatever anchor was keeping me connected to the earth has come loose, and now I'm floating away, but nobody even knows I'm gone. Home isn't here, not in this half-built tent, not in this place full of friendly strangers. Home isn't even in Seattle, not at my parents' house, not in that place full of unsaid things. I wonder if it'd be different if this isolation were what I was raised to be used to. Like you, who has felt like an alien in your family since the day you were born, who's never felt like you were at home anywhere. Maybe you're the lucky one for not having expectations.

When we were kids, you always said you were jealous of my family. You'd stay over at my house as much as you could. We'd fantasize about my parents adopting you, of us being sisters, of you never having to see your dad and step-mom and half brother again. But that all stopped last year. Suddenly your house became the better place to stay.

With you around, I don't have to think about these things. But without you here taking up space, without your voice and your needs and your big dramatic feelings, all that's left is me. Everything around me is quiet. The only things to hear are the thoughts inside my own head.

So I take a nap. I lay out a towel and stretch out on the

cot and try not to think about what else has happened on it. I trust sleep to silence me for a little while.

I wake to the dinner bell ringing in the distance. I feel sticky, and for a moment I don't know where I am. "Sadie?" I say, but you are not there.

At dinner, I sit with Beverly and Simon and their seven-year-old son, Micah. I have never met such a well-behaved kid in my life. He sits there, calmly eating his food, listening to us talk as if he's actually interested. During a lull in the conversation, he announces, "I love kale!" and I can't help but laugh my amazement. They tell me how they met in college in Colorado and ran a vegetarian restaurant for a few years before coming here. We don't talk about much of importance, but it's nice to have a conversation without some kind of drama attached to it. I realize that it's the first real conversation I've had with anyone besides you since we got here, not counting that awkward exchange with Lark at the clinic. I look around the patio and realize I haven't really talked to any of these people yet; I don't even know most of their names, even though we've already been here well over a week. Up until now, you have required all of my attention. We've worked by ourselves in the fields rather than join the others. We've stayed isolated on our remote edge of the lake. The only social contact we've had is at mealtimes, and even then you always choose the least crowded table, and we always leave as soon as Doff announces the next day's assignments. All this time, we've been surrounded by all these nice people, and we know none of them.

I want to stay. I want to play board games and try Ezra's homebrewed beer with the others after dinner. But I make you a plate and fill a thermos with tea. I rush off without saying goodbye.

"Hey, Max!" I hear someone yell after me. I turn around and see Maria waving. "Where are you going? Don't you want to hang out?"

"I have to take this to Sadie," I say, holding up the food and tea as evidence. "I'd love to, I really would."

"Okay," she says. "Tell Sadie we all hope she gets better soon. And one of these days I'm going to kick your ass at Scrabble." She turns and runs back to the house, long skirts flowing behind her, and I want to follow her. I want to let her kick my ass at Scrabble. I want to throw this food in the bushes and forget about you for one night. I wasn't brushing Maria off, but I have enough experience to know how people give up after you've turned them down enough times. People at school who have invited me to do things, guys and girls who have asked me out on dates—after the second or third declined invitation, they all give up. *I have plans with Sadie,* I'd always tell them. *I'm doing something with Sadie.* Sadie, Sadie, Sadie.

As I walk the path to the trailer, I realize I'm nervous. About what, I don't know. Nervous to see you? Nervous about you seeing me?

When I knock on the door, you don't respond. I open it slowly and step inside. It is stuffy and smells like sweat and bad breath. I open the windows and prop the door open. "Sadie?" I whisper. You don't move beneath your pile of blankets. I set the plate and thermos down on what used to be my bed.

"Sadie."

"Mmmmm?" you mumble into your pillow.

"I'm going to take the beanbag chair," I say. "And a couple of pictures. Okay?"

"Mmmmkay."

"How are you feeling?"

You roll over onto your back and look at the ceiling.

"I brought you dinner," I say.

You don't respond.

"You'll never guess where I'm staying," I say. You remain still, but your eyes shift to finally look at me.

"Why aren't you talking?"

You point to your throat, then motion like you're strangling yourself.

"Oh," I say. "I'm sorry. Do you want some tea?"

You nod and sit up. I hand you the thermos. You try to

open it, but you're too weak, so I do it for you. I pour you a cup. I sit on my old bed as you take little careful sips.

"Can you talk at all?" I say.

"Yes," you croak. "A little. But it hurts."

"Do you need some more Advil?"

You nod. The open bottle is sitting on the bedside table within your reach. I move to get it for you, but something stops me.

"It's right there," I say.

"Oh." You reach over and get it yourself.

I look around the room as you take the pills. Everything is in the same place as it was before, but it seems like everything has changed.

"I miss you, Max," you say, your voice surprisingly normal despite the pain you claim to be in.

"I miss you, too."

"I hate being stuck in here. It's like I'm in prison."

"It's a nice prison, though."

"I guess." Your eyes drift off to somewhere in the distance.

"It looks weird from the other side of the lake," I say.

"Will you bring me some new books tomorrow? I'm so bored." You are staring at your wrist, poking it with your finger.

"They couldn't have put me any farther away," I say.

"I think my wrists are losing weight."

"Guess who's my new neighbor?"

"Is that possible? Can wrists even lose weight?"

"Sadie, are you even listening to me?"

You look up like you finally just noticed I'm here. "Huh?"

"I'm staying in the yurt next to Dylan," I tell you. "We're, like, next door neighbors."

Your eyebrows narrow into a frown.

"The yurt isn't even finished, but I guess it's the only place they had left to put me. It's crazy; I can practically see into his cabin from my window."

Your fingers tighten around the bottle of Advil. I feel the room get suddenly hotter. I imagine the lake outside boiling in sympathy with you, steam rising, scorching the earth around it. You glare at me with fire in your eyes. I cannot remember you ever looking at me like this.

"Sadie, what's wrong?"

"Fuck you."

"What?"

"Fuck you." You throw your blankets off your shoulders. All your fatigue and weakness is suddenly gone. "How can you come in here and say something like that?"

"Like what?"

"You're just shoving it in my face."

"Shoving what in your face?"

"'Oh, Sadie, you'll never guess where I'm staying,'" you mock. "'Oh, Sadie, you'll never guess how awesome life is out there. You'll never guess what a great time I'm having while you're stuck in here.'"

"I didn't mean it like that."

"Whatever, Max."

"I'm sorry." I can hear my voice getting higher. I can feel the tears pushing at my eyes. "I swear, I didn't mean it like that. I'm so sorry."

If it is you who is hurt, why am I the one crying?

"I'm sorry," I say again. I keep saying it over and over. I've been saying it forever.

But what if I'm not sorry?

"I'm going to go now," I say.

"Fine." You cross your arms at your chest. "Go."

What if I have nothing to be sorry about?

"Don't be like this," I say.

"Be like what?"

"It's not my fault you're sick. Don't take it out on me."

You pull the blankets back up around your shoulders.

I can feel you watching me from your corner as I collect the beanbag chair, a vase, and a couple of framed pictures off the walls.

"Can you close the windows before you go?" you say flatly.

"Don't you want some fresh air?"

"No."

I close the windows.

"I'll bring by some books tomorrow," I say. "Is there anything else you want?"

"My life," you say. "I want my life back. Can you get me that?"

"I don't think so," I say. I walk out the door and close it behind me.

Νάρκισσος

NARCISSUS

In myth, you are a man. Your name means numb-ness. You know you are beautiful, and when you look into some-body's eyes, it is only ever to see yourself; eyes are nothing more than glassy pools, just a surface to reflect you.

There are so many who have loved you, so many you have scorned, so many echoes of heartbreak. So many whispers pack-aged into a scream you still can't hear. Those who love you are destined to waste away, to crawl into some hidden darkness, fad-ing until they become only withered voices repeating what you say. You are followed by a trail of suicides, but you never look back.

Here is your pool, this lake surrounded by echoes. Here is the end of the line. You lean over the water, a glassy sky. Here is your reflection; the funhouse mirrors turn you into infinity.

Here is the beautiful girl staring back at you, the only one you can possibly love. You are thirsty, but you won't touch the water, won't dare destroy your image with cruel ripples.

But water arms do not hold. You cannot kiss your own reflection. You cannot drink beauty. So you die and are replaced by a flower—beautiful but useless.

I have discovered a kind of rhythm without you. It's nothing profound, but it's consistent. I dig and I pull and I pick and I sow, and that's all there is. Simple. Peaceful. You would call it boring. And maybe boring's nice for a change.

But it's strange swimming without you. That is when I miss you most. I float after a long day of work, and the lake seems so much more vast, so much deeper. I am always too far from shore. I hold the air in my lungs, trying to make myself more buoyant, but the water seems less willing to hold me. The field may be my place, but the water was always yours.

It's the time between the after-work swim and dinner that I find strangest, when I feel the most lost. I towel off and put on clean clothes, but then I have nowhere to go. It's too hot to stay inside my yurt, and I have no shade outside. If I go up to the house, someone will give me work to do in the kitchen. As tired as I am, that's what I usually end up doing, even though all I want is to sit down and stretch my legs in the shade and read or nod off for a few minutes. But that is not an option. I have three choices: sit in the sun, sit in the hotbox of my yurt, or work in the kitchen, where there's at least a fan.

I'm sitting in my doorway, hoping this time will be different than all the others, that maybe I'll finally feel a breeze that will make this position bearable. But no. The air is still festering with heat. I'm already drenched with sweat, even though I just got clean.

And Sadie, there you are, across the water. I can see you looking out your window. The trees behind the trailer protect you from the afternoon sun, and for a second I feel a twinge of jealousy at how cool it must be inside. You are bathed in shadow, you have not worked for days, and I know these things mean nothing against your fever and quarantine, yet I can't help but want what you have. I wave. I can't make out the look on your face as you wave back, but I can read so many things into the way your hand moves—the stiffness of your wrist, the lack of enthusiasm. Then you close the blinds, and I'm alone again.

I haven't seen you in three days. Skyler begged to take your meals to you, and I saw no reason why not. But now I realize you must be wondering where I am, why I haven't come to see you. And I guess I am wondering the same thing. I am wondering why it has been so easy to let you go.

I cannot work in the kitchen. I cannot bear to stand up, cannot bear to do anything with my hands. Even chopping vegetables seems impossible. Even peeling garlic seems like too much work for the tiny muscles in my fingers. But I cannot stay here in this excruciating heat. There must be an option I have not thought of yet. If anything will lead me to it, desperation will.

I look all around. Maybe there is some piece of shade that I missed, a tree previously hidden. But just like before, all the trees are on your side of the lake. And all the porches are on other people's houses.

Yes, there it is, my new option: a porch on someone else's house.

I look to my right, and there is Dylan. Even stretched out completely he would not take up his whole porch. He could fit two of me on there with him. He has shade to spare. And this is a commune, isn't it? Isn't everyone here supposed to share?

It looks like he's sleeping. He's lying on his back with his arms behind his head and a baseball hat covering his face. It's not fair that he gets to be this comfortable during the hottest part of the day. I haven't seen him step foot in the fields or lift anything heavier than a plate, and yet there he is taking a nap. I'm just hot and tired and grumpy enough to not care that I'm terrified, so I pick up my book, slip on my sandals, and limp my way over to his cabin.

"Hey," I say. He doesn't move. "Hey," I say again, trying to sound like you when you get anything you want.

He finally stirs. He pulls the hat off his face and squints to see me against the sun. "Hey, what?"

"Can I sit here?" I say, trying to do that inflection you do that makes questions sound more like commands. "I have no shade at my place."

He looks around, like he just noticed that he is, in fact, lounging in the shade. He looks at me skeptically. "What are you reading?" he says, like he's asking me for the password to sit on his porch.

"*On the Road*," I say. "By Jack Kerouac." I hold my book up as evidence.

"Yeah, I know who the author of *On the Road* is." He squints even more as he studies me, and I have never felt more judged in my life.

"Kind of cliché," he says. "A high school kid reading

On the Road." He scrutinizes me some more, and I hold my breath as I wait for his verdict. "But at least it's not a romance novel or that young adult shit," he finally says.

"There are some really good YA books," I say, momentarily forgetting to keep my cool. "There's even a National Book Award for young adult novels. That's pretty legit, don't you think? Have you ever even read one?"

He frowns, and I'm pretty sure I blew it and he's going to kick me off his porch any second now. But finally he sighs and says, "Sit."

So I sit. I lean against the side of the cabin and stretch my legs out. A light breeze blows, but the physical relief I wanted so badly is now compromised by a new tension. I'm not sure how I'm supposed to relax being this close to Dylan.

"What are you reading?" I say.

"You wouldn't know it."

"Try me."

"Wittgenstein."

"That's a philosopher?"

"Yeah."

"Why do you read so much philosophy?"

"I like to know how people think."

"But that's not really how people think," I say. "It's only how one guy thinks people think."

He looks at me like he's surprised, like it just dawned on him that I exist. "Huh," he says, and looks back at his book.

I try to read, but it's impossible. I look across the lake, but your curtains are closed. I wonder if you're on the other side, peeking through a tiny hole that I can't see.

"What are you doing here?" I say. I don't know what's gotten into me. I have always been the quiet one. You have always been the talker. But you are not here.

"What do you mean, what am I doing here?' he says. "I'm sitting on my porch trying to read a book."

"No, I mean here on this farm. What are you doing in the middle of Nebraska?"

"I'm just working like everyone else."

"But you're not like everyone else here," I say, and as soon as it comes out of my mouth, I feel my face burn. It must sound like I've been paying attention, like I've been thinking about him enough to decide what he's like and not like. "What I mean is you're not a hippie really. You don't really seem like the commune type."

One side of his mouth turns up in a smirk. "Oh yeah?"

"Yeah," I say. Neither of us says anything for a while, but it seems like he's laughing at me somewhere inside.

"What do you even do here?" I ask.

What am I doing? Max, shut up.

"Same as you," he says. "Same as everyone. I work."

"But what *kind* of work? You don't do any farming."

"There's more to the farm than just farming."

"Like what?"

"Administrative stuff," he says. "Running errands."

"So you're like the secretary? Like the errand boy?"

He smirks again. I have a feeling I'm nowhere close to guessing what it is he does here.

"Sure," he says. "Whatever you say."

The sun gets lower in the sky, and people are moving toward the main house. They've been here so long they know what time it is without the dinner bell telling them.

"But why here?" I say. "You could do that kind of job anywhere. Why did you come all the way out here?"

"I don't know," he says, looking out across the water. "It's *away*."

"Away from what?"

He turns and looks at me. For the first time, he looks me in the eye. His eyes are piercing blue: not a sweet kind of blue, not like sky, but more like ice—sharp. They seem to look right through me, into my brain and down through my heart, into my stomach where he can see the butterflies in their frenzied flight. "Away from everything," he says.

"What are you trying to get away from?" I say, my voice almost a whisper.

He looks into my eyes with that smirk that until now seemed so cruel. But there's something else in it, something playful, something that makes the butterflies go ballistic. He tilts his head and says, "What are *you* trying to get away from?"

The bell rings in the distance. "It's time for dinner," I say.

"So go to dinner," he says, still looking in my eyes.

"Aren't you coming?"

"I'm not into crowds."

"Okay," I say, not moving.

"Bye," he says, picking his book back up, resuming his place like nothing happened.

"Bye," I say, barely managing to pull myself up. I concentrate as I descend the stairs from his porch, fully aware that if I were to trip and fall in front of him, now would be the perfect time.

I walk to dinner, take my plate, sit next to new people I don't know. I think I join the conversation, but I can't remember what we talk about. I stay up at the house after dinner, joining a game played on a converted Monopoly board, except they've renamed it "Collective" and changed the rules in some confusing way to make it less capitalistic. I go through the motions of being involved in whatever's happening around me, but really I'm just replaying the few minutes on Dylan's porch over and over in my head, looking for meaning, innuendo, anything to make it something bigger than it was. I keep looking around for him, waiting for him to arrive for dinner, but he never shows up.

"I'm going to go keep Sadie company," Skyler announces in my general direction.

"Honey, I'm not sure you should be spending so much time with her," Skyler's mom says. "What she has is really contagious."

"Don't worry, Mom. I'm being careful," Skyler says with her chin in the air. "She really needs a friend right now." She looks at me with the brattiest look an almost-thirteen-year-old could possibly give.

Sadie, I should probably visit you tomorrow.

"Skyler, you have such a beautiful, generous heart," her mom says with a big embrace.

The guy with the phoenix tattoo grunts, and it's nice to know someone thinks this exchange is as ridiculous as I do.

When I leave the house to walk back to my yurt, people hug me goodnight like we're family and won't see each other for a long time. With each hug my tension eases, and by the end I am hugging back. I can't remember the last time I really felt part of something, felt part of a group that was bigger than two people.

"I'm glad you stuck around tonight," Maria says with a goodnight squeeze.

"Me too," I tell her.

It feels like midnight, but I know it's only about nine thirty. I light my lamp and try to read, but my mind can't focus on the words. So I turn it off and just lie there in the dark, listening to the music the night makes, the crickets and birds and mysterious other invisible things. It is so big around me, the millions of little voices taking up space, making themselves heard, all of them so much louder than the tiny size of their bodies. Sadie, it sounds so different on this side of the lake without you next to me.

Dylan is only a few meters away, separated by air and a couple of thin wooden walls. He is probably lying in bed just like me, hearing the exact same sounds. His breath is so close, I am probably breathing some of him in. He is breathing some of me. And the lake is a barrier, a fence between your world and ours.

Sadie, maybe this story isn't about you anymore.

Part II

The gods have no mercy for the hero.

They swat her around like bored cats with a spider.

This is the thing about will—one can always choose not to play. But the tragedy of no is the refusal of maybe. It is saying "the end" before even getting started.

Say yes. Open your eyes and find yourself lost.

Step forward. Weave your way through the labyrinth with your frayed ball of string.

I cannot tell her story if I am not in it.

Time stops.

Blank pages.

Stars dance in each other's orbit, spinning faster and faster until they lose control.

There are two choices: fuse together or fly apart.

In one part of the world, she is sleeping.

In one part of the world, I am not.

Once upon a time.

After four days of avoiding her, I am finally bringing Sadie breakfast. The first thing out of her mouth is, "Where the hell have you been?" and it goes downhill from there.

"I've been busy," I tell her. As soon as I say it, I know it is the exact wrong answer. "I mean, Skyler really wanted to bring your meals," I try to correct. "She was begging me to let her do it."

"So you could have come with her. And there are other times of the day, you know," she says. "You could have visited me anytime."

"I know," I say. "I'm sorry."

Neither of us says anything for a while. Her hair is even crazier than usual. It sticks out in all directions in stiff faded-pink tendrils. I can see how some caveman long ago would have been inspired to invent Medusa—facing a woman like this, full of rage and with snakes in her hair.

I remain standing as Sadie throws herself onto her couch throne. My beanbag chair is across the lake. My place here is gone.

"How are you doing?" I say.

"How does it look like I'm doing?" She sighs, lifting her legs up like they weigh a million pounds. "I'm miserable."

"I'm sorry," I say because I can't think of anything else.

"Stop saying you're sorry."

I almost say *I'm sorry* again, but I catch myself just in time. "Is there anything I can do?"

"Tell me a story," she says, closing her eyes. "Tell me what's happening out there in the world."

"I'm not in the world either, Sadie." My voice is sharper than it should be. "I spend eight hours a day in the sun, pulling weeds. Most nights I go to bed before it's even dark. Trust me, you're not missing much."

She stares at me. "Why are you being so mean to me?" she whines, her face getting red the way a baby's does before it starts to cry. She's lying on the couch like a lazy princess while I stand in front of her like a maid waiting for instructions.

"How am I being mean to you?" My voice is shaking, and

my hands are fists. "I've been working my ass off to make up for you."

Her face is twisted into a caricature of someone being hurt. "You're mad at me for being sick," she whimpers dramatically.

"No, I'm not," I say, but my voice is full of anger.

"Yes, you are."

"I don't want to fight with you." But I do. I do want to fight. All I want to do right now is fight with Sadie. But instead I say, "I have to go." It's a lie. I have nowhere to go. "I have to get to work."

"Whatever." Sadie crosses her arms like a stubborn child, and I think hanging out with Skyler has caused her to lose a few years in maturity.

"Bye, Sadie," I say, walking out the door. "I'll come see you soon." I don't wait to hear her response. What is wrong with me?

I don't know what to do. I finished all my jobs two days ago and no one's given me a new one. Everything that needed to be harvested is harvested and everything that needed to be planted has been planted, and I'm stuck here with nothing. Yesterday, I at least got to tag along with Maria on daycare duty while people finished the last of the farm duties before break. It was nice hanging out with the kids, drawing pictures, playing hide-and-seek and looking for bugs all day. I don't have any little brothers or sisters, but I know Sadie's half brother well enough, and I've done my fair share of babysitting, and I have to say that, by comparison, these kids are awesome. For one, they don't have a nervous breakdown every time they're asked to share. They're confident and funny and creative, and don't seem plagued by the ADD all the city kids I know seem to have. Maybe I'm biased, but I have a feeling these kids are a lot less likely to grow up to be high-strung assholes than their urban counterparts. And they probably won't need as much therapy.

But everyone is off today, and all the kids are gone. Everyone is with their families, taking a few days' vacation before the next round of work starts. I should be hanging out with Sadie, I should be with my best friend, but all I want to do is be as far away from her as possible. I don't know where it's coming from, but I have this feeling all of a sudden like she's poison, like being near her sucks something out of me, like *she* sucks something out of me, and I only now realized it's something I want to keep. And I'm alone with all these feelings swirling around with nowhere to go, and I need someone or something to distract me, but there's nothing. Even the breeze has died, and the birds are holding their breath, testing me with their silence.

I stomp up to the main house because I don't know what

else to do. I wish the dogs were at least here to talk to, but they always follow Doff wherever he goes. Only Sadie has ever loved me that much, but it was me who did the following, me chasing her around with my stupid wagging tail. But now what? I'm stuck, alone, in this deserted place. I am walking toward an empty building. Maybe I'll read a twenty-year-old *National Geographic*. Maybe I'll play a board game with a ghost. Maybe I'll sit perfectly still and let the spiders wrap me up and push me into the corner with the rest of their cobwebs.

When I get there, the place is empty. A couple of lazy flies circle the living room. Around and around and around, looking for something that isn't there. I hear the mumble of two low voices from up the stairs, where the offices are located, and my breath catches in my throat when I realize how grateful I am to be so close to other humans. Footsteps bring them closer, but I still can't make out what they're saying. The stairs creak as they descend, and the voices stop suddenly as two figures come into view. There are Dylan and Old Glen, looking at me like I've interrupted something important. They are not happy to see me, but I want nothing more than to hug them. I just want someone, anyone, to touch me and remind me I exist.

"Hi," I say, trying not to sound as pathetic as I feel.

Dylan nods the way cool guys do, like he doesn't want to waste energy on recognizing my existence. Old Glen breaks into a big smile, as if that was his mood all along. "Hi there, Max!" he says, a little too enthusiastically. He looks like a farmer Santa Claus with his gray beard, his big belly protruding from his stained overalls.

"Hi," I say again.

"Uh oh," Glen says. "You look bored."

"Maybe."

"It must be rough to have your friend out of commission."

"Yeah."

"I've heard good things about your work."

"Oh." All I can manage are one-word answers. Anything else and I think I'd start crying.

"I hear you're a really hard worker," he says. "You have a natural knack for farming."

"Oh," I say. "Thanks?" I've never been good at talking to adults. Or kids. Or really anyone besides Sadie.

"Why don't you go run errands in town with Dylan today?" Glen says. "Get out a little."

"What?" Dylan snaps. "No."

An axe makes a clean chop through my chest.

"Come on, Dylan," Glen says. "There's plenty of room in the truck for Max."

"Glen," Dylan says, looking at him too seriously. "I really don't think that's a good idea."

"Don't worry," Glen says, walking over and patting me on the shoulder. "I'm sure Max here will be fine company."

Dylan looks at me like I've already done something to piss him off. I am doing everything I can to keep from bursting into tears.

Glen whispers something to Dylan that I can't hear, then leaves. "Meet me at the green truck in five minutes," Dylan tells me flatly.

"Okay," I manage to say.

I walk out to the truck. I close my eyes and take deep breaths. Two thin wet streaks sneak out of the sides of my eyes. When they reach my chin, I wipe them off with the back of my hand. My face is dry. I take a deep breath. I tell myself there will be no more tears today.

Dylan drives, and I stay silent. But after fifteen minutes of no talking and no radio, I can't take it anymore. I need to talk. I need to do something to keep me from thinking. "Where are we going?" I say to the silence.

"Columbus," he mumbles.

"That's far, isn't it?"

"Pretty far."

"Is it a big town?"

"Big enough for fast food."

No one says anything for a minute.

"What does that mean?" I say.

"What does what mean?"

"What you just said. 'Big enough for fast food.' Is that, like, a saying?"

"Not that I know of." I can't tell for sure, but I think he might be hiding a smile. The edges of his mouth are definitely higher than usual. Being on the road, away from the farm, seems to have relaxed him. Something inside me lets go.

"Then why did you say it?" I say.

"Because there are fast-food restaurants there."

"Why does that matter?"

"Because that's why we're going there."

"We're going to fast-food restaurants?"

"Yes." He's definitely smiling. He's enjoying my confusion.

"Why the hell are we going to fast-food restaurants?" I nearly shout with frustration, but I feel giddy at the same time, like there's this sweet, tight electricity in my chest, in my stomach, lower. We're having an actual conversation.

He smiles so big he shows actual teeth. This is the most animated I've ever seen his face. I don't know what happened, but he's like a completely different person all of a sudden. "Because we're collecting their used deep-fryer oil," he says. "It's what we use to make our biodiesel. It's what our trucks and generators run on."

"Why didn't you just say that the first time?"

Am I flirting?

"It wouldn't have been nearly as much fun."

He said fun. He called this fun. He thinks *I* am fun.

"Jesus," I sigh.

"Jesus has nothing to do with this."

I smile. Dylan is smiling too. I have felt too many things in the last thirty minutes, and I want this one to stay. Please, let this feeling last. Let Dylan not be the asshole I thought he was. Let him be just one of those people with the kind of super-dry sense of humor where you can't tell when they're joking. Let me be the one who knows him well enough to know when that is. And, please, let him like me.

"So that's what you do?" I say, trying to sound normal. "That's your job at the farm? Making biodiesel?"

"That's one of my jobs."

"What are some other ones?"

"Whatever comes up."

"Like what?"

"Like driving bored girls around, apparently."

"I'm moral support," I say.

"Sure."

"You need it," I say. "People get cranky when they're alone too much."

"Are you cranky?"

"A little. Are you?"

"Probably."

We drive mostly in silence the rest of the way there, but it's the most exquisite silence I have ever felt. A few times, I even catch myself smiling in the side mirror. The sun warms my face but the breeze through the open window keeps it cool. I close my eyes and feel it brush against my skin. When I open my eyes, I catch Dylan looking at me. He looks away quickly, but I can still feel the burn of his gaze, printed onto my skin, making me beautiful.

I barely even think about Sadie.

The town isn't anything special, but it's definitely bigger than Hazeldon. I'm surprised to find myself annoyed by the streetlights. The sidewalks and neon signs seem offensive. A car honks and shatters the pleasant buzz of the drive. Dylan is all business as we stop at each restaurant to pick up the used oil. His smile is gone as he tells me to stay in the truck. Everything smells like old French fries. Just like that, things change again and I can do nothing about it.

"This is the last one," Dylan says as we pull into a chain burger place. He looks at me as he turns off the truck. "Thanks for your patience." A tiny hope blinks again inside me. "Are you hungry?" he says. I nod. "Want a burger?" I nod bigger.

"Come on," he says, and I jump out of the truck and follow him in.

He exchanges handshakes with a middle-aged man with shifty eyes and a badge that says MANAGER. I sit in a booth by the window. Dylan places our order with a pimply cashier while the manager stares at me with a lecherous sneer. I look down at the table, try to push him away with my mind. Dylan and the man talk a bit more, and I can tell they're speaking in low voices, leaning into each other so no one will hear. Why would they need to be this secretive about used French-fry oil?

"What kind of pop do you want?" Dylan yells across the restaurant.

"Surprise me," I say. The manager has returned to his lair in the back and I feel better. Dylan brings our food over on a plastic tray, and the smell of trans fats and preservatives makes my mouth water.

"Pop?" I say, grinning. I snatch my food off the tray.

"That's what they call it here."

"It sounds like something a cartoon would say." I rip my burger open and take a huge bite. I've been eating organic vegetables and whole grains for way too long. "Oh my God, this is amazing." I chew with my eyes closed.

When I open my eyes, Dylan is staring at me.

"What?" I say.

"You're something," he says, then finally takes a bite of his burger.

"What does that mean?"

"Nothing," he mumbles with his mouth full.

Once again, my feelings have turned full circle in just a few minutes, and I am floating. I stuff my face with fries, and I'm pretty sure this is one of the best meals of my life. We don't talk while we're eating, but it feels somehow intimate, like we're getting to know each other by seeing how the other person consumes food. I watch his Adam's apple drop when he swallows, watch his jaw flex sharp and strong as he chews, and I never knew eating could be so sexy.

When we're done, I hop into the truck, but Dylan stays back. "One second," he says.

"Okay." I put my feet up on the dashboard, pleasantly full and a little sleepy.

He walks up to a back door next to the Dumpster and knocks. The creepy manager pokes his head out and holds the door open with his shoulder. He pulls a wad of bills out of his back pocket and hands it to Dylan. They shake hands and the manager gives me one last leering look before he shuts the door behind him.

"What was that?" I say when Dylan gets in the truck.

"What was what?" he says.

"What were you guys doing?"

"Nothing. Just saying goodbye."

"But he gave you money."

"Yeah. For the oil."

"Shouldn't you be paying *him* for the oil?"

"He's paying me to get rid of it."

I look at him hard for signs of a lie, but I don't know him well enough to read his face. I'm used to Sadie, who can't hide anything, but Dylan is impossible to read. I think I could study him for years and still not know what he's thinking. I decide to leave it. I don't want to risk my feelings changing again.

We drive and drive. There is something comforting about Dylan's silence now. It's not awkward like so many other silences.

"So, how'd you become best friends with the classics department at Oxford?" he says out of nowhere. At first, I have no idea what he's talking about. But then I remember Sadie's bragging, her special way of saying everything in half lies.

"Oh, that. It's not really as exciting as Sadie made it sound. My mom got her PhD in history there and stayed close with one of her professors. He ended up becoming head of the classics department, so I guess that means I have a pretty good in."

Dylan's quiet for a while, then says, "Seriously, why classics? Of all the things in the world to study. Why something so dead?"

"It's not dead," I say. "It's the foundation of Western civilization."

He smiles but says nothing. For some reason, I want to tell him things. "I grew up listening to my mom tell me the old stories and myths," I say. "They're a part of me."

"People grow up listening to all kinds of stories, but that doesn't mean they all want to spend their whole lives studying them," he says, but there's no cruelty in his voice. "Why do those stories mean so much to you?"

"I don't know." I realize I'm telling the truth; I've never asked myself why they mean so much to me. "Like some people are fascinated by the human mind," I begin, not knowing where I'm heading. "So they become therapists to understand what makes people work. I guess it's kind of like that, but instead of psychology or science, some cultures used all these myths and symbols and poetry to explain the human condition. And instead of a medical diagnosis for one of our bizarre behaviors, they have a crazy god or a goddess or monster to make sense of it. And they told these stories for thousands of years, and the stories changed as the culture changed. They were these living, breathing things—their stories, their explanations. To study a culture that understands itself through imperfect gods—it's fascinating. I mean, what would we be like if we thought our gods were even more dysfunctional than we are?"

Dylan has that subtle grin on his face. It is so slight, most people might not notice. It is so rare, so special, I feel proud when I earn it.

We sit in silence for a while, the imperfect gods passing between us.

"So, what does your mom do with a PhD from Oxford?" he finally says. The gods tense; they turn sinister. Then just like that, they are gone.

"She used to be a professor," I say. "At the University of Washington." How can a conversation turn so quickly?

"Used to be?"

I say nothing. This is where the conversation ends.

"Did she . . . die?"

I shake my head.

"Sorry," he says. "I didn't mean to—"

"It's okay." My mind is blank. All feeling moves downward. The French fries and fast-food meat have finally found my stomach. I feel sick.

"What does your dad do?" I can tell Dylan's trying to sound cheerful as he changes the subject, and part of me softens.

"He's a lawyer."

"What kind?"

"Family law."

Dylan opens his mouth, then closes it. After a pause, he opens it again. "I used to want to be a lawyer."

And just like that, the air shifts again. It buzzes between us, full of promise.

"What happened?" I say carefully, not wanting to break the spell.

"I realized college wasn't for me."

"Why not?"

"Full of too many college students," he says with his grin.

"That's not a real answer."

His raises his eyebrows at me like he's surprised I caught him.

"You're tough," he says.

"So, what was wrong with college?"

"I don't know. Maybe I'm not the kind of person who does well with structure."

"Or maybe you found out you weren't as smart as you thought you were."

He snaps back as if stung. I went too far. His lips tighten into a straight line. Two conversations ended within a minute. All the unsaid things fly out the window.

"You're different," he says, staring ahead. The deep green of the farm comes into view.

"How?"

The Oasis sign welcomes us home. I feel a sudden panic, like my time is running out. Dylan doesn't say anything, just leaves my question hanging lonely in the air. We drive all the way up the driveway before he answers.

"You're not full of shit," he says.

"Um, thanks?"

"It is a compliment."

"Okay."

He parks the truck and turns it off. We sit in silence. I feel like I'm supposed to say something, but I have no idea what.

"We're here," he says. Neither of us moves.

"It was nice talking to you," I say. It's the most talking I've done since Sadie got sick, the most talking about myself in what seems like years.

"Yeah." He pauses for a moment before he opens the door, like he's thinking of saying something more. But he doesn't. He steps out of the truck and closes the door behind him, leaving me in here alone. I would feel insulted if anyone else did that, in any other place, at any other time. But I'm pretty sure I just experienced Dylan being nicer to me than he is to anyone, and I'm pretty sure I'm the happiest I've been in a long time. I'm not going to let a little slammed door bother me.

"How do you feel about goats?" Doff asks me over breakfast.

"I've never really thought about them," I say, scraping the last of the oatmeal from my bowl.

"Feel like taking a break from vegetables? I need some help with the animals. Old Glen said he could spare you."

"Okay," I say. "Sure." Come to think of it, I could use a break from the vegetables. They're not the most exciting of company.

"Lulu's about to give birth any day now," Doff says proudly. "So that should be pretty exciting."

"Where does she go?" I ask.

"Where does who go?"

"Lulu," I say. "To give birth. Do you take her to the vet?"

Doff seems confused for a second. Then he laughs his honking laugh as soon as he realizes I'm serious. "*We* deliver her," he says. "You and me."

I feel the blood drain out of my face.

Doff looks worried. "Do you think you can handle it?"

For a moment, I'm afraid. I imagine blood and guts and horror-movie gore. But then I realize we're talking about something natural, something that's been happening for millions of years before me and will continue to happen long after I'm gone. I have no reason to be afraid of it.

"Yeah, what the hell," I say. "What else am I going to do?"

We finish breakfast, and I follow Doff and the dogs on the long walk over to the barn. It's been a few days, but I still haven't told Sadie about the biodiesel run with Dylan. I haven't told her about how sitting on his porch has become an afternoon ritual, *our* afternoon ritual. And even though we don't really talk, we're still together, sharing space, intentionally. These are the kinds of things you're supposed to talk about with a best friend, but I don't want to tell her any of it. And I feel guilty for that, but at the same time it is somehow freeing to finally be the one with the secrets. Still, I can't believe she hasn't noticed, hasn't peeked out her window and looked across the lake to see me sitting next to him, hasn't smelled the residue of desire still on my skin when I visit her.

Work's picked up, and everyone's busy again. I've been visiting Sadie at the trailer after dinner with Skyler. We play cards or a board game, Sadie and I barely talking while Skyler narrates with her constant monologue, as if she's been saving up things to say for years. It's strangely fascinating to listen to her stories of what it's like being "that Oasis girl," how she's picked on at school for her mismatched clothes and vegetarian lunches, how she doesn't have any friends her own age. She's out of school for the summer and doesn't have much to do besides a few chores, so she's been spending her days with Sadie. When I arrive after dinner, it's like I'm a guest in their weird little world. I can't help but feel that I've been replaced by this almost-thirteen-year-old, and I think I should feel sad about that. There's a twisting in my chest that could be sadness. It could be jealousy. Or it could be something else entirely.

I can smell the animals before we get there, a smell like wet dog mixed with shit and sawdust. But there's something sort of comforting about it, as if it triggers an ancient instinct in my genes, an evolved affinity for domesticated beasts. A big red barn rises up from the fields, a gate open to the gravel road on one side, the remaining three sides spotted with smaller doors, all exposed to the fenced-in acres where the animals live. It's like Noah's ark or a giant petting zoo; there are animals every-where, of all kinds. Cows, sheep, goats, and pigs stand around or wander leisurely, chomping on grass like chewing gum, eyes droopy with relaxation. There's an occasional *baa* or *moo*, but nobody seems like they have too much to say. They don't seem to notice the chickens pecking obsessively around their hooves; they pay no attention to the ducks quacking orders like little generals; they regard Doff's spastic dogs as if they're sugar-high children. All the farm sounds collect into their own little symphony. The sun shines, the white clouds float lazily in the sky, and I feel like I'm in a nursery rhyme.

"Bella," Doff says to a brown cow with huge udders. "This is Max. Max, this is Bella."

"Nice to meet you, Bella." She sniffs me with her big nose, her nostrils twitching.

"She likes you," Doff says, then laughs his honking laugh. The dogs jump like lunatics.

The barn is cool inside and very quiet. All the animals are outside, so their little pens that line the walls are empty. "They come in here to sleep," Doff says. "Like clockwork every night. The sheep go in this one." He points to a pen to the left with a sheep-sized opening to the field. "The goats go in this one. The chicken coop's around the other side, next to the rabbits."

"Rabbits?"

"Yep, bunny rabbits. We have to keep the boys and girls separate because, well, you know about rabbits," he says with a wink.

"And here's Lulu!" Doff announces as he walks me to the other side of the barn. In another pen is a black goat with a big round belly, backed into a corner and breathing heavily. "Isn't she beautiful?" Doff says as he opens the fence and slips into the pen with her. She baas gently as he approaches, as if politely asking him for help. He crouches down, leans his head against her belly, and rubs her neck. "What do you think, Lulu?" he says softly. "You got a couple kids in there? Are they ready to come out?" She baas forcefully in response, a definite yes.

"Is she okay?" I say.

"Yeah, she's fine." He pulls her away from the wall. "Let's just see what's going on back here." He looks at Lulu's backside and breaks into a big grin. "Okeydokey," he says. "Looks like Lulu's going to be a mama any second now."

"What's happening?"

"The girl's in labor already. It's your lucky day, Max. Come in here."

"In there?" It feels off-limits, like I'd be intruding. Like something special's happening that I don't deserve to be a part of.

"I'm scared." The words catch in my throat, so much heavier than they sound, so much bigger than this moment.

He gives me a big warm smile. He thinks I'm only talking about the goats. "You're going to be great," he says, and I decide in that moment to believe him.

I enter the pen as Doff turns Lulu around. A wet bubble is protruding from her, like a see-through balloon full of dirty water. I step back. "What is that?"

"That's the placenta," Doff says. "Sometimes it likes to start coming out before the kid does. But see that little hoof there? Look a little closer."

I step forward and peer into the baseball-sized sac like a crystal ball. Sure enough, there's a tiny hoof in the middle of it, as big as a bottle cap, connected to a leg that is still mostly inside Lulu. A small voice tells me I should be disgusted by this, I should be running as fast as I can back to civilization. But I am surprised to realize there is nowhere I'd rather be but here. I stare at that hoof and a sweet warmth spreads through my body. Lulu cranes her neck around and looks at me. Her eyes are pleading for good news.

"It's okay, Lulu," I say, rubbing her rump. "You're doing great."

Doff smiles. "Here we go."

I stand behind Lulu while Doff crouches in front of her, cooing encouragement. I have a feeling she doesn't really need us here, that she's perfectly capable of doing this on her own;

she's doing us a favor letting us hang around. I don't tell Doff this. I think it would break his heart. He's over there beaming like a proud father, like he has something to do with this, like this is his accomplishment too.

"Oh my God," I say. Lulu pushes and the hoof turns into a leg. She pushes again and now there are two legs. "It's coming," I say.

"Good girl!" Doff says. He rubs her belly. She makes horrible noises, almost human noises, and I can tell she's in pain, but there's strength in her voice too, power. Doff whispers, "Push," and she grunts. The tiny legs turn into a body. Lulu pushes and pushes, and the body grows longer. I realize my face is wet with tears. "It's almost out," I say.

"Catch it," Doff says.

"What?" I feel dizzy. I back away, rest my arm on the fence for balance.

"You're doing great," Doff says, and I can't tell if he's talking to me or the goat. "Just breathe," he says, and I do.

"Okay," I say. "I'm ready. I'm here."

"Catch it," Doff says. "Open your hands. Hold on to the body. Help her ease it out."

My fingers wrap around the warm, squirming wetness pulsing with life. Lulu pushes and the baby shudders with her force. I squeeze with the slightest pressure, feel the fragile body in my hands. I pull as gently as I can, and I feel the pressure release as the head slides out. The placenta ruptures in my hands and sends warm, thick fluid gushing around me. But I am not thinking about that, not thinking about the mess, not thinking about something that will have to be cleaned up. I am holding a brand-new life in my hands. It feels like the only thing that exists, like all that matters is in this little squirming bundle, and yet the world seems suddenly so much bigger, my place in it so much more tangible and real.

"Oh, wow," I think I'm saying. "Oh wow, oh wow, oh wow." I'm staring at a tiny, perfect face with still-closed eyes, a little mouth opening and closing with its baby voice, a warm just-born body in my arms, all black with a little white circle on the top of its head like a halo.

"Put it down, Max," Doff says gently. "Let Lulu meet her baby."

I rest it down as softly as I can, its legs still tangled, and Lulu starts licking it immediately, already a mother, already knowing exactly what to do. "It's a girl," Doff says, though I have no idea how he can tell. "Congratulations!"

"Congratulations, Lulu," I say.

"Do you want to name her?" he says.

"Me?"

"Yeah, go ahead."

"Artemis" comes out of my mouth. The goddess of animals. The goddess of birth.

"Well, that's dramatic," Doff says, chuckling. "Artemis it is. Welcome to the world, little Artemis."

Lulu baas again, and Doff goes to her. "Get ready, there's another one coming."

"Artemis, you're going to have a brother or sister," I say.

"Lulu, you have got to be kidding," Doff says, then laughhonks uncontrollably. The dogs bark outside the pen, jumping so high their heads pop up over the side, one and then the other, again and again. "Get it?" Doff says, slapping his knee. "*Kidding?* Baby goats are called kids. Lulu's *kidding.*"

"Oh my God," I say. "That's awful." But I'm laughing too. The dogs keep hopping up and down like a pair of synchronized jack-in-the-boxes. Lulu looks at us like we're crazy, but we keep laughing through the second birth, as Doff tends to Lulu while I guard Artemis, making sure Lulu doesn't accidentally step on her. It's only my first day, and we're already a good team, Doff and me.

The second one is also a girl, a photo negative of her sister—all white with a black spot on the top of her head. "Look at that," Doff says. "I've never seen anything like it." He places them next to each other and Lulu gets to work licking them clean.

"They're perfect," I whisper.

"The second one needs a name too," Doff says.

"Penelope," I say immediately. It is my mother's name.

The smell of birth is overpowering. This is what life smells like—blood and pain and love.

I help Doff clean up the pen and lay fresh straw. We wash our hands at the spigot outside, then lean on the fence of the pen watching as the babies figure out how to nurse.

"She's going to be a good mom," I say.

"I think you're right."

I know all I really did was stand there. All I did was catch something that would have found its way to the ground without me. But I can't help but think this is the most important thing I've ever done.

"Thank you," I say.

"For what?"

"For letting me be a part of this."

"You're very welcome." He puts his arm around my shoulder and squeezes, and a knot of sadness and yearning tangles around my heart. Doff's arm is the same weight as I remember my father's, whose arm I have not felt in a very long time.

"You did a great job," he says. "You're a natural."

"Really?"

"Oh, absolutely. I can tell the animals trust you. You calm them."

"Thank you," I say, and this approval feels somehow so much more important than any grade I've earned or Latin test I've aced. Standing here in this barn, covered in slime and smelling of manure, I feel more alive than I have in a long time. I wonder what would my life look like if it weren't on paper, if it weren't contained in the safe world of dusty stories. What if I replaced the old gods and heroes with something more tangible, something with breath I can feel, eyes I can look into, fear I can soothe, pain I can relieve? What if I chose a life that's a little more bloody and alive?

"Do you have kids?" I ask Doff.

"Nope."

"Why not?"

"Never got around to it, I guess."

"Do you regret it?"

He smiles. "Maybe a little."

"You would have been a good dad."

He looks at me, his face a mix of surprise and gratitude. "What a nice thing to say."

I shrug, suddenly embarrassed for speaking so openly.

"Well, I got these crazy dogs," Doff says, bending down to hug them close. "They're like my babies." They lick his face, their tails wagging like crazy. Artemis and Penelope are sleeping now, nuzzled against their mother. "Why don't you go take a shower and relax a little before dinner?" Doff says. "You've had a big day."

"Dinner," I say. "What happened to lunch?"

"We worked through lunch," he says. "It's been about three hours since the bell rang. You didn't hear it?"

"Holy crap."

"Time flies when you're pulling kids out of a goat's ass," Doff laughs, and the dogs laugh with him. I feel like I'm floating as I walk back to the house.

Despite the concrete floor and mildewy walls, that shower is one of the best showers of my life. Sweat and dirt and the remnants of Lulu are washed away, and I feel so much cleaner than I do after my usual dips in the lake. Someone else enters the stall next to me, but I think nothing of it. I've gotten used to these close quarters, used to moms whipping out breasts at the dinner table to feed their babies, used to seeing middle-aged folks swimming naked. But as I'm collecting my stuff to leave, I am definitely not prepared to see Dylan emerge from the shower with a towel wrapped around his waist, dark hairs wet against his skin on his chest and trailing down under his towel. The air gets sucked out of my lungs. The room is suddenly tiny. I can feel the heat coming from his body. There are only a few inches of air between our skin.

"Oh, hey," he says.

"Hey." I cannot look him in the eye.

He is facing me. I could reach out and touch his chest. I could pull away his towel, leave him standing there naked. I can hear myself breathing. I am practically panting. I am an animal in heat.

"Uh," I mumble. "I gotta go." I grab my stuff quickly. I have to get out of here. I have to leave before I attack him.

"Bye," I hear him say behind me, and I swear there's a smile in his voice.

Ἄρτεμις
ARTEMIS

Some call her style justice; others call it revenge.
But language of course is only a tool, impartial to our whims—
semantics know no morality. Everyone is one or the other: object
or subject, masculine or feminine. This is the business of words.

Regardless, she was made of gold.

Upon birth, she was already a midwife. Her tools: an elk
horn, a boar's tusk, the whispered song of arrow feathers. She was
born owning the moon.

She will find you in the forest. She will teach young girls to
run barefoot over pine needles, how to hunt with bow and arrow,
how to shake the mountains, how to talk to beasts. She does not
know how to lie.

Of the gods' many paradoxes, this is the one consistency: There *is always a catch to freedom. Her rules are specific: Love a man and you are dead to her.*

Bring your dolls, your toys, your childish things, and leave them at her altar. Give back your weapons and map of the woods.

Then walk away in shame at being tamed.

As lonely as I've been, I don't feel like being around anyone tonight. Is this what turns people into shutins? Realizing that everyone they know just disappoints them?

When you experience something amazing, aren't you supposed to want to share it with someone? Is that what normal people do? I did experience something amazing today, but I don't want to share it with anybody. I don't want to give it away. I want it to be mine, just mine. This is such a different feeling than I've ever had. I always felt a compulsion to tell Sadie everything, as if I needed her witness to make it real.

I run up to the house and get in the dinner line. I try not to make eye contact with anyone, try not to invite conversation. Maybe if I keep my head down, I can stay invisible. This is something I've always been good at. But as soon as I get my plate, Skyler appears by my side. I am instantly anxious.

"Sadie's got strep throat, you know," she lays right in.

"What?"

"You were gone," she says smugly. "Her temperature was a hundred and three, and she couldn't swallow. *I* went with her and Lark to the clinic."

"Good for you," I say.

"Aren't you worried?"

"About what?"

"About Sadie? About how she has strep? She's on *antibiotics*."

"That's good, right?" I say. "That'll make her better."

Skyler stares at me like I'm speaking Swahili. She can't understand why I haven't dropped my plate of food and started weeping over Queen Sadie.

"You can't visit her," she says. "She's sleeping. The doctor says she needs to sleep."

"Okay." I grab a fork and put it in my pocket.

"Don't you even care?" Skyler says.

"Of course I care."

"You're acting like you don't care."

"I'm tired, Skyler. I've had a long day."

Her face wrinkles into a mask of confusion. It relaxes in a

moment of recognition, then turns into a triumphant smile. Skyler has just realized I have surrendered my position as Sadie's attendant, that it's all hers.

"Bye, Skyler," I say.

Maria and Joseph invite me to have dinner with them, but I tell them I want to be alone. I actually say it—I don't lie, I don't come up with some excuse. I just tell the truth, *my* truth, and they say okay like it's no big deal, like it's perfectly reasonable to want to be alone sometimes.

I eat quickly, balancing the plate on my lap while sitting at the door of my yurt. The sky is perfectly clear tonight, as it is most every night. There are so many stars here, more than I've ever seen, and they reflect off the lake. If I squint, I can almost believe I'm surrounded. Sadie's windows are dark, and I can almost believe she's not there.

I hear footsteps. No one ever comes this way. This is the end of the trail. No one ever comes out here except me and Dylan.

He appears, lit blue with moonlight. His head is cocked to the side, his footsteps unsure. "Hey," he says, holding up two bottles of beer in one hand, a flask in the other.

"Hey," I say.

"Don't tell me you're turning antisocial like me," he says, slurring a little.

"Are you drunk?"

"'Drunk' is a relative term." He sits next to me in the doorway, his leg brushing mine. He hands me a bottle of beer. "Here," he says.

"Thanks," I say, taking it. "Do you have a bottle opener?"

"Watch this," he says, grabbing the bottle from me and taking a lighter out of his pocket. After a few clumsy maneuvers with the bottom edge of the lighter, the bottle cap pops off. "Ta da!"

"Congratulations," I say, smiling. As much as I don't want to be around people tonight, I guess I still want to be around Dylan. Maybe because he's so mysterious, because there's so much still left to know. Or maybe because he's incredibly hot.

He passes me the flask. "What is it?" I say.

"Whiskey," he says. Sadie's favorite drink. I take a swig, and it burns just like I remember. I hand it back, swallow some beer to wash the taste away. But it's still there, branded into my throat.

We sit there for a while in silence, looking out at the lake. I'm afraid to look at him, so I stare at the water, waiting for something to change, waiting for something to break the stillness. Nothing happens.

"I got to help deliver two baby goats today," I finally say. "Doff let me name them."

Dylan takes a big swig of the whiskey. "Oh yeah?" he sputters in that choking way people talk after they drink a shot. "What'd you name them?" He takes a swig of beer to wash the whiskey down.

"The first one is Artemis."

"Artemis!" He spits out the beer. It sprays out of his mouth into the darkness. I hear it splat against the dirt. "Are you a lesbian?"

"What?" I say, trying to hide the hurt in my voice with anger. "What the hell is that supposed to mean?"

"Artemis is a pretty dykey name," he says, passing me the flask. I swat it away with my hand.

"I can't believe you said that," I spit. "You're such a dick."

"What'd I say?"

"'Dykey'?" I can hear my voice rising. "Just because we're in Nebraska doesn't mean you get to be a homophobic asshole. It's not just some word. It's not like saying 'pop.'"

He laughs like drunk people laugh. "Oh my God, you're so mad!" he says.

"Of course I'm fucking mad!" If I were a cartoon, there'd be steam coming out of my ears. I want to punch him. But I also want to jump in his lap and stick my tongue in his mouth. I don't know how I'm supposed to have these two feelings at the same time.

"Chill out!" he gasps, sucking in air to catch his breath. "My sister's a dyke. That totally gives me permission to say it."

"No, it doesn't," I say, but I sigh inside with relief that maybe I don't have to hate him.

"I call her a dyke all the time," he says. "She loves it."

I can't decide if I should pretend to still be mad at him. Will I lose something by giving up this easily?

He leans over and bumps my shoulder with his. A wave of electricity burns through me. "So, are you?" he asks. "A dyke?"

"I'm bi," I tell him, and I'm surprised by how easily it comes out. I turn to look at him. He's smiling. Something inside me turns soft.

"That's cool," he says.

"Don't get all pervy on me."

"I'm not! Jesus, you don't have a very high opinion of me, do you?"

I shrug, trying to act cool, but I can't stop the smile creeping onto my face.

"My ex-girlfriend was bi," he says.

"Yeah? What happened to her?"

"She dumped me for a chick."

"Oh," I say. "I'm sorry."

"It's okay," he says. "I would have dumped me for that chick too."

"What was so great about her?"

"Who?"

"The girl she dumped you for."

He looks me in the eye, smiles a sad kind of smile I have never seen on his face. "She wasn't me," he says.

"Oh."

The air is charged with something new.

"So what'd you name the other one?" he says. "The other goat?"

"Penelope."

"Is that some feminist icon I should know about?"

"It's my mom's name," I say.

"You named a goat after your mom?" He laughs. "That's kind of cold."

Something inside me twists up again and closes.

"Hey," Dylan says. He reaches out his hand and wraps it around my cheek, gently turns my face toward his. "Sorry," he says. "Sorry." He drops his hand, puts it back safely in his lap.

I want to tell him. I want to tell someone. It's dark and quiet and we're at the end of the world, and maybe if I say it here, in the middle of nowhere, it won't be so real in my head anymore.

"She hasn't been doing too well lately," I say. His sudden kindness eggs me on. "She got in an accident about a year ago and shattered her spine. She's in a wheelchair now, and the doctors say she can get around if she wants to, and we even got the car all customized so she can drive it."

Dylan says nothing. He just waits. It is up to me if I want to speak or be silent.

"She could work now if she wanted to. She could have a lot of her old life back. That's what we keep telling her." I look at Dylan and he's still there, still listening. "She was on a lot of medication." I stop here. I don't know where else to go.

"What kind of medication?" he says.

"I don't know."

Across the lake, Sadie's trailer is still dark. I have an urge to jump in the lake with all my clothes on and let the water wash all of this off me. But all of a sudden a white light slices across the sky, like God cut the night open just for us.

"Holy shit!" I say. "Did you see that shooting star?" I point at the sky even though it's long gone. I look at Dylan, at his signature half smile. "Did you see it?" I say.

"How cliché." His eyes pierce into mine. "Talking to a pretty girl and seeing a shooting star."

I'm glad it's dark, because I know my face is red. But the night is so quiet he can probably hear my heart pounding in my chest. I want to pretend he didn't say what he just said. I want to tuck it away to think about later, when it is safe, when he's not sitting right here beside me.

"Why is everything always cliché with you?" I whisper. I think my lungs have deflated. I can't get any air.

"I don't know," he says. "Nothing surprises me anymore."

The moon sparkles in the dark pools of his eyes. Stars are falling all around us, little sparks, little shocks of electricity.

"So, you want to be surprised?" I say. I am leaning in. He is leaning in.

"Yes," he says. "Surprise me."

My mouth on his. The taste of beer and whiskey. The first thing in my head is this is what Sadie's mouth must taste like to all the boys she's kissed.

I push the thought out. She does not belong here. This is not about her. Nothing has to be about her anymore.

My eyes are closed, but I can still see the stars. I am floating. The stars swirl around us. They light upon my body, and I can feel each and every one, millions of them. I can feel the softness of hands searching my body, the pressing of fabric, fingers searching for a way under, then warm skin on mine.

Stars everywhere, but something like a dark blankness in front of me, a thick, impenetrable cloud attached to my lips. Something doesn't feel right, like Dylan is only half here, like an important part of him is missing. Maybe because he's so drunk, half of him is already passed out. As soon as I realize this, the stars dim and I pull away. He's still there, eyes closed, lips parted, like he hasn't even realized I'm gone, like he fell asleep midkiss.

"I'm tired," I say. It takes him a moment to register my voice, then he nods.

"I'm going to bed," I say. His eyes open to drowsy slits.

"Going to bed," he says.

"Alone." Even though I'm hot and melted, even though my skin is still stinging, waiting for his hands.

He stands up, wobbly, like Lulu's babies when they took their first steps, like being drunk has made him forget how to walk. He knocks over the beer bottles, and the clinking glass is shockingly loud in the darkness. "Oops," he says, and continues walking to his cabin. He leaves the spilled bottles for me to clean up. He does not say goodbye.

Part of me is still buzzing, pained at his absence, wanting to follow him into the night. But part of me is relieved he's gone. This is the part of me that wants to breathe, that wants things to stay manageable, that knows he is trouble. But sometimes the body is stronger than the mind. Tonight the mind won, but just barely.

Ἀφροδίτη

APHRODITE

Born of sea foam, she came to Earth surfing a shell. Born of castration, she was perfectly aware of what she did to men.

She was born already a woman—already wanted, already claimed. She already smelled of sex. Tiny cupids circled her like flies, drawn by the fishy scent.

She never tasted a love which did not require her naked. Perhaps this is what made her so bitter, what made her search for love so crazed and desperate. The hole of her childhood filled with fury, and she punished those who did not love her enough. Anything less than worship was blasphemy. Her vanity spun tornadoes; her yearning planted wars.

A goddess can still be wounded. In the middle of battle, she *can wince in pain and run off in fear. She can become just like the ones she scorns, abandoning those she claims to love, leaving them on the battlefield to fight for her, alone.*

Was it she who cursed Medusa's hair? Was Medusa beautiful before she became a monster? Is jealousy strong enough to make snakes?

Of course, the goddess claimed that famous apple, the trophy that named its owner most beautiful. She was the original wicked stepmother.

Mirror, mirror, on the wall, who is the fairest of them all?

I float through my days, watching Artemis and Penelope grow stronger. Doff convinced Old Glen he needed me full-time at the barn, so now I am spending my days with the animals, and they're the best company I've had in a long time. I feed them. I milk Bella. I collect eggs in a cushioned basket hanging from my arm. Doff doesn't say much, and neither do the animals. We're comfortable in each other's company, peaceful in our silences.

Some of it is hard work. I have to clean the pens and shovel manure into a wheelbarrow, then drive it out to the giant compost bins that turn garbage into fertilizer for the farm. I end the day covered in shit, my muscles burning. But there is a weird satisfaction in being part of this cycle, of doing my job to ensure nothing is wasted. It's not lonely like being out in the fields. The animals keep me company, taking turns walking over to sniff me and rub against my legs. They don't demand anything, don't suck me dry with their insecurities and dysfunctions. They are so much less complicated than people, so much more forgiving. All they need is food and water and some space to walk around in. Like people, they make messes that need to be cleaned up, but their messes are so simple, so honest, so much less taxing than the ones people make.

I refuse to give Dylan's kiss credit for my mood. I don't want to believe he's that powerful. Yes, maybe I woke the next morning giddy. Maybe my stomach jumps every time I think of his mouth on mine, his warm hands under my shirt. Maybe I've been searching for him in the three days since that night, showing up on his porch every afternoon like clockwork, looking for him in the house at every mealtime, knocking on his door every night. But it's like he disappeared into thin air. One night, he's kissing me; the next morning, it's like he never existed. The green truck has been missing too. When I realized this, I had a moment of panic. Maybe he left. Maybe he's gone for good. But then I climbed a couple of milk crates to peek into the window of his cabin, and it looks like his stuff is still there.

Is this normal? To sneak around looking for a boy you kissed once? Sadie always says you know you're doomed if you find yourself thinking about someone when they're not there. That means they have the power. That means you've made them more important than yourself. She says that's when you know you have to get rid of them.

But what does she know about love?

Sadie's fever has finally gone down and I'm going to visit her. I am thinking of telling her about Dylan. The morning after we kissed, I suddenly missed her; I missed having a best friend to tell things. That's what I'm telling myself anyway. But maybe part of me wants to show off. Maybe part of me wants to hurt her. Maybe I'm not as good as we've always thought I was. I've always lived in comparison to her, and she was always the wild one. But since she's been gone, I'm starting to wonder if maybe I'm a little wild too.

But when I get to the trailer, I lose my nerve. Lark is there, doting on Sadie way too enthusiastically, like she's making up for all those years of lost time. It's a cacophony of "Can I get you this?" "Can I get you that?" and Lark flitting around the cabin like a tornado of guilt. Sadie's upright, her eyes so much more alive than they've been since she got sick, watching her mother's inspired performance. Her hair is still a mess, and she's as pale as she gets during the winter in Seattle, but she seems oddly content, like she is finally being rewarded for her suffering.

When Lark runs up to the house to get some more tea, Sadie starts weeping. She grabs my hands and hugs them to her chest. Her skin is cool for the first time in weeks.

"Oh, Max, it's so wonderful!" She is like something out of a Victorian novel, with her sickbed swooning.

"What's wonderful?" I say, shocked by the coldness in my voice. "Being sick?"

"My mom," she says. "She's been so great. We had a really good talk on the way to the clinic, and she was crying and I was crying, and she apologized for everything and promised to make up for it and be a better mother."

"Wow," I say, unimpressed.

"It's everything I wanted."

"What about Skyler?" I say. "Wasn't she there too? Wasn't that kind of awkward?"

"Oh, Skyler." Sadie laughs. "We just ignored her. She was fine."

She is holding my hands, but I feel no connection to her. I have a strange feeling like my hands are just a prop.

"It's kind of fun having someone worship you," Sadie continues, so much like her old self. "It's like having my very own slave. She'll do anything I tell her."

I draw back my hands. I suddenly have no desire to touch her.

"Did I tell you about the crap her mom was giving me? Some stuff called flower essences where they put some flowers in water and pretend it's a magic healing potion. Antibiotics are way better, believe me. I'm feeling better already. Seriously, Max. I'm coming back, like, really soon. Can you believe it?"

No, I can't believe it. I want to cry, to scream, to punch a pillow, anything. I am furious. I am a terrible person. Evil. I don't want Sadie to get better yet. I don't want her to come back. I just started being okay without her.

"That's great," I say, but she is so enamored with herself she doesn't even notice my half-assed lie.

"Where is Skyler, anyway?" Sadie says. "She was supposed to give me a massage tonight."

"What's that quote about power corrupting?" I say, grinding my teeth. There is gravel in my voice.

"Huh?"

"'Absolute power corrupts absolutely,'" I say. "Who said that?"

"What are you talking about?"

"Nothing."

Sadie laughs. "I think being alone has made you a little crazy."

I will not tell her about Dylan. Let her think whatever she wants. Let her think I've been lost without her. I don't care.

"You're right," I say. But I am lying. Being alone hasn't made me crazy. If anything, it's made me more sane.

When Lark returns with the tea, it's obvious Sadie's done with me. She has a new favorite now.

"I'm going to bed now," I say.

"Good night," Lark and Sadie say in unison, then turn to each other and giggle at their synchronization.

As soon as I leave the trailer, I feel a weight lifted off me. It's only around Sadie that I feel so heavy. Everyone else here— Doff, Maria, Joseph, all the kids—they demand nothing from me that I don't want to give. They give me my own space to be sturdy. With Dylan, it's the exact opposite, but in a way even nicer. With him, I feel weightless, like I can't even feel my feet on the ground. Part of me suspects this may not be a good thing. But part of me doesn't care.

I decide to go up to the house one last time before bed. A few people are still on the patio, passing around a joint. They see me coming and try to hide it.

"It's okay," I say. "I won't tell on you." It's pretty comic, adults trying to hide their pot smoking from a teenager. Somehow it doesn't seem so illicit here. How much trouble could a few stoned people really get into in the middle of a farm?

I poke my head into the kitchen. No one is there. Most

people have gone to bed by now. I climb the stairs and see a light on in the office. Maybe Dylan's there, doing his mysterious "administrative" work. I feel my heart pounding as I approach the slightly cracked door, and I hear typing on the office computer. I knock softly and push the door open. "Hello?" I say, and I can hear the hope burning in my voice.

"Hello?" It is not Dylan's voice. I open the door to find Old Glen, his long gray hair hanging down the back of the office chair. He spins around and greets me with a grin. "Hi there, Max," he says.

"Oh, hi," I say, doing little to hide my disappointment. "I thought you were Dylan."

He chuckles like a movie Santa Claus. "I'm afraid I'm not that young and strapping," he says.

"Do you know where he is?" I say, trying not to sound too interested. "I haven't seen him the last few days."

"He's been out making deliveries. He should be back tomorrow afternoon."

"Oh," I say. I want to hug him for that news, but I restrain myself. I feel like I should say something else, but I don't know what. "Well goodnight then," I finally say.

"Goodnight, Max."

As I walk back to my yurt in the darkness, I remember that

a man named Tim is the one who usually makes the vegetable deliveries in a big white van. I wonder what other deliveries Dylan could be making with the green truck.

But who really cares? Not me. All I care about is that Dylan's coming back tomorrow.

It is June 21. The summer solstice. Apparently this is a big deal for hippies. It's like the biggest hippie holiday, as important as Christmas is for people who like to shop.

Dylan was supposed to be back by now. I've been hanging out around the house all afternoon waiting for him, even though I knew that meant I'd get roped into helping get ready for the party. So instead of swimming or taking a nap after shoveling shit all day, I'm moving chairs and hanging lights for a party I don't even want to go to.

As I'm arranging dried wildflowers in canning jars for centerpieces, I feel a hand on my shoulder. My breath catches. But I turn around and it's just Lark.

"Hi, sweetie," she says.

"Hi."

"Thanks for helping."

"No problem."

"Hey," she says, leaning in like we're conspiring something. "Don't tell Sadie about this, okay?"

"About what?"

"The party. She's almost well enough to start getting back to normal, but the doctor says to give it another couple of days to make sure her fever's down for good. She's already chomping at the bit, you know?"

"Uh huh."

"There's no way she'd stay put if she knew there was a party."

"Okay."

"You're great, Max," she says, squeezing my shoulders.

"Thanks?" I say, but she runs off before the word has time to reach her.

The weirdness of this place has grown on me, and I've found that I like quite a lot of it, but tonight takes it to a whole new level. As much as she's pissed me off lately, I really wish Sadie were here for this. I so badly want to hear her running commentary; I need her laugh right now. But instead I have to sit here and watch the madness unfolding, alone in my witnessing quite possibly the strangest party I have ever seen.

The night starts normally enough with dinner, except

everyone's dressed up. And by "dressed up," I mean they look like something out of a Harry Potter movie, with long flowing dresses and robes. The women and kids all have ribbons and flowers in their hair. Old Glen is wearing a blue robe and some kind of horns on his head. His dinner prayer is longer than usual. He goes on and on about abundance and purification and positive energy, and all the adults are nodding and closing their eyes meaningfully, and all the kids are running around like lunatics.

After dinner, Old Glen lights a big bonfire by the lake, and a bunch of people start drumming. The kids run around the fire while the adults take turns throwing in herbs and saying prayers under their breath. I'm sitting off to the side, watching it all from a safe distance, and I'm pretty sure my mouth is hanging open in shock. Doff is banging on some bongos and doesn't look quite as crazy as the others, but most everyone else is spinning around in circles with possessed looks on their faces.

I so wish Sadie were here. I consider going to get her, dragging her out of the trailer in her smelly pajamas so she can witness this. She would love it. We'd have weeks' worth of material to laugh about. I'm just about to get her when I see Lark in the corner of my eye, away from the group, in the shadows of the trees on the right side of the lake. Marshall is holding her hand, and I can tell they're giggling. They look back at the crowd one last time before they run into the trees. I look at Doff and he is happily drumming away, completely oblivious to Lark's betrayal, and I want so badly to hug him, to let him know someone thinks he's wonderful. Now I definitely can't get Sadie. The first thing she'd do is look for her mother. And knowing Sadie, she would probably find her.

Maria and a few other parents start rounding up the children. Old Glen says something about the holiness of youth, and everyone waves goodbye to the yawning children as they're led to their beds. As soon as they're gone, people start passing around clay bowls full of some kind of hot tea. Old Glen throws some herbs in the fire and calls on the magic spirits to lead them safely into the other dimension, and that's when I decide it is definitely time for me to go.

I walk down the path toward my yurt as the intensity of the drumming increases and the group starts chanting. Without someone to laugh with, the night is just embarrassing instead of funny.

As I'm passing Dylan's cabin, I hear a "Psst!" My heart jumps in my throat. I peer into the darkness and see his outline in the shadow of his doorway, camouflaged by the night.

"Hi," I say. I take a few steps in his direction.

"You're not enjoying the party?" he says. I can hear the smirk in his voice.

"Are you serious? I think they've all lost their minds."

"Yep," he says.

"What are you doing?" I say, stepping closer. I can make out the details of his face now. His sharp features emerge from the darkness.

"Watching," he says. I turn around to face the direction he's facing. I see the bonfire lighting the sky, the figures dancing around it. Bats dart around them, and the scene looks like something out of a fairy tale.

"They look like witches," I say.

"They *think* they're witches." Dylan laughs. "But they're a bunch of middle-aged, out-of-touch fools."

"They're having fun," I say, feeling a little protective of them.

"Have a seat," he says, and I enter his darkness without hesitation.

As soon as I sit, he hands me his flask. I take a swig and feel the whiskey burn down my throat.

"I think they're on something," I say. "They can't be sober and do that without laughing."

"Mushrooms," Dylan says.

"What?" I say. "I was kidding."

He chuckles. "Seriously. Psilocybin. Did you see them passing around some tea?"

"Yes."

"Did you drink any?"

"No."

"Do you want to?"

"No."

Maybe.

"I have some," he says. "Enough for both of us."

"How'd you get it?"

"Secret."

"You have a lot of secrets."

"I also have a lot of mushrooms."

I've been looking for Dylan for days, but now that he's here I don't know what to say to him. I don't know that I even want to talk. I just want to be near him, to feel him next to me.

"Well?" he says. He pulls a plastic sandwich bag out of his pocket. It is full of gnarled brown twig-looking things.

"What do they taste like?"

"Honestly, they taste like shit," he says. "But we have this to wash 'em down." He holds up the flask, full of whiskey that also tastes like shit.

I sigh. What the hell? I've spent my whole life being careful, haven't I? I've always been the one to make sure everything's under control. But what if I don't have to be that person anymore? What if I get to be the crazy one for a change? What's the worst thing that could happen?

"Fine," I say. "Just a little."

The mushrooms really do taste like shit. I gag with every swallow. Dylan laughs at me.

"Am I done yet?" I choke. "How many do I have to take?"

"That should be good," he says, then throws an extra handful in his mouth. "Yummy!"

We sit there for a minute watching the bonfire in the distance. "Now what?" I say.

"You have to wait."

"For how long?"

"About an hour."

"An hour!"

"Are you in a hurry?" he says. "Do you have someplace you have to be?"

I don't respond. What are we going to do for an hour?

We sit. And we sit. It seems like forever. "How long now?"

"Jesus, girl," Dylan says. "You seriously need to work on your patience."

"I'm bored."

"Boredom is not very Zen."

"Who said I was Zen?"

"Patience, grasshopper."

"Where were you?" I say. "The last few days."

"Around."

"Around where?"

"Around Nebraska."

"Around Nebraska doing what?"

"Delivering."

"Delivering what?" I hear my voice rising. I think Dylan enjoys doing this to me. He enjoys being infuriating.

"Things."

"What things?"

"Secret things."

"Fuck you!" I say, and I shove him. He falls over and starts laughing, faceup on the ground.

"Ooh, you are so tough," he mocks, grabbing my wrists and pulling me down. I am lying on top of him. My face is so close to his I can feel his breath on my lips. If this is his version of foreplay, this insulting me and making me mad, it sure seems to be working.

"I am tough," I say.

"Of course you are." And he pulls me tight against him.

We kiss. And we kiss. Somehow he ends up on top of me. I don't know how long we kiss, but pretty soon it turns into something else, something not kissing, something even better, and suddenly it's like my whole body is kissing him, like every pore of my skin has its own pair of lips.

"Oh my God," I breathe into his mouth.

"Do you feel it?" he whispers.

"Yes," I say. "I feel it."

I feel it like a sound in my body, like a vibration, like God is playing music through me, and it sounds like these kisses, and I am the music, and Dylan is an instrument, and we are playing together. We play and we play, and the crescendo shakes the earth, and suddenly we are so loud the whole universe can hear us. All the gods have perked up their ears. They find us by the light of the bonfire. And they join our singing with their own, but theirs is so much bigger, so much louder, and it enters us, and I don't know where the gods stop and I begin, and it's too loud inside my body, the vibrations are too strong, and I have to make the music stop, I have to turn it off, I have to come up for air, I have to breathe, so I break away, I stop singing, I open my eyes and it is dark.

"I'm blind!" I scream.

"What?" Dylan says, and he sounds like he's still in me.

"I can't see!"

"Open your eyes." His voice a cacophony, like out-of-tune violins.

"They are open! I can't see. Everything is black!" I am falling. I hear the *whoosh* of gravity around me. I am scared. I am going down and down and deeper and deeper, into the earth, into this giant body, and the music is too loud, it sounds like rocks breaking, like mountains dying, and I shouldn't be here, I'm not ready. I'm not ready.

Then stillness. I'm in a tunnel. Where is Dylan? Where is the bonfire? Where is Sadie? I'm too alone. I know the ground was on my back once. I know a boy was on top of me. But now I'm in a cave of earth. I'm still blind. I reach out my arms and feel wet mossy rock around me. I walk, but I don't know if I'm going forward or backward. It's cold here. I'm sick. I'm full of poison. The pressure of the walls around me squeezes it out. It squeezes and squeezes until there's nothing left. I taste the poison in my mouth. I hear it. It is coming out of my stomach, through the tunnel of my body. It is out. I am empty. I am clean.

"Gross!" someone says at the end of the earth. I follow the voice.

"Let's get out of here," I think I say.

"Chew this gum," the voice says. An offering on my tongue, a sacrificial wafer. The ritual of receiving. The taste of a clean soul.

"Thank you," I say. "Amen."

And then we run. The tunnel is long but I am fast. The rock turns into a labyrinth, a maze of corn like they have at

Halloween, but this one's like a woven basket all around us. I still can't see, but I can feel the tall stalks slapping my face. I can hear my body thrashing through them. I can hear the sad souls hiding behind them, everywhere I turn, broken spirits lost in the maze, moaning ghosts guarding the tunnel. But because I'm blind, I can't see them and I'm not scared. They can't trick me with their pyrotechnics. I know I can pass right through them. I know they're no match for me.

We wander for hours, days, years, eons. We are holding hands. We are on this journey together. Then in the darkness comes a light. A tiny pinprick on the horizon. God poked a hole in the tunnel just for me. I let go. I am running toward it. The light is mine. It was made for me. It was put here to teach me something. I know that now. All this time I've been running, I haven't known what it was for. I only knew my feet had to keep moving, even though I was tired and sick and wanted to sleep, to float, to have the darkness take me. But here's what I have to do. I have to follow the light. I pass all the lost souls. I untangle myself from their grabbing hands. I follow the light and find the one I'm looking for.

Mother, you should not be here. You are not dead yet. I know your body is still alive, even if you wish it weren't. You are only part dead. You are only visiting here. This is not a good place for a vacation. This place is work. You thought you could come here and mingle with death. You thought you could hide from life in the darkness. You thought you could be safe here from pain. You thought no one could find you.

But here I am. I have found you. You ran from the world when your legs stopped working, but I can run faster. I escaped the tunnel. I caught the light. I caught you. But now maybe I'm stuck. Maybe I went too deep. Maybe the tunnel is closed, the ghosts built a wall of sadness to trap me with you.

"Dylan!" I cry.

"What?"

"Are we stuck here? I don't want to be underground."

"We're in a cornfield, Max. Open your eyes."

"I want to go home."

"Calm down. It's okay. Trust me. It's okay."

"I don't want to be stuck."

"We're not stuck. This is freedom. Don't you see?"

Freedom.

What if I just let go? Let go of everything, let go of myself, let go of you, let go of everyone I try to love, let go of everyone I want to love me? What if I just gave up trying to clutch everything so tight? What if I let go of the fear of losing it all? What would be left? What does the soul look like when it's alone, without all its ornamentation? What do we look like without all these illusions we attach to ourselves to make us look bigger?

I am big enough.

This soul. This perfect, pure thing.

I am enough.

I open my eyes and everything is clear. The night is still, and there isn't a cloud in the sky. I am surrounded by corn. I may be lost, but I am not scared. Nowhere is always somewhere if I am in it.

Dylan is behind me, thinner and lighter than I've ever seen him. He is not as strong as I thought, not as sharp. I realize now his coolness is an act, a costume stitched out of fear. Now here he is in front of me like a wet cat, his fur flattened to show how small and how vulnerable he really is. I see him for the first time. He is lost like me. He is terrified. He is running, reckless, from himself and into nothingness. I don't want to follow him. I don't want to go where he's going. But maybe I can help him, maybe I can pull him in the other direction. Maybe he needs me like Sadie needs me. Maybe I can keep him safe. Maybe I am the strong one.

He reaches out his hand for me, and I take it. I put my arms around him and squeeze, feel his frail, brittle bones against mine. I will take care of him. It's what I'm good at. It's what he needs.

"I'm okay," I tell him.

"I thought I lost you," he says.

"I think the road is this way," I say into the night. I turn around. I start walking. I follow our trail of destruction through the corn. Dylan follows, not letting go of my hand. We reach the road and the sky opens up. The world is huge, and I am in it. From here, I can see everything. I see the bonfire of the farm. I follow the light back.

We don't speak on the way there. Dylan is lost in his own internal darkness. I am taking him to the light. The night bugs cushion the air with their song, and I feel safe in their company, safe in my own skin. I survived. I have earned my place here among the living.

We reach the main house and everyone is gone. The fire is almost out.

"How long were we gone?" I say.

"Forever," Dylan says.

He takes my hand and leads me to his cabin. We squeeze into his small bed. I am not nervous, not scared. He is a boy now, not a man full of sex and destruction. He falls asleep with me rubbing his back, the way I used to rub Sadie's back when she drank too much, the way I rubbed Lulu's stomach when she was giving birth, the way all living things want to be touched when they are scared and breaking. Now I have claimed him with this soothing. I have made the magic to calm him. My arms have kept him from falling apart. He is mine now. He is mine.

The chaos of the night falls away as my breath joins his. In and out. In and out. Our breath is the only thing that exists. It is the only song I hear. There is nothing to be scared of as long as we keep breathing.

Part III

Romulus and Remus were the kind of twins who were already fighting in the womb. Not like Castor and Pollux, the other famous pair—bound by a love so strong they became a constellation.

Sometimes orphans turn feral. Sometimes they are suckled by a she-wolf. Sometimes they acquire a taste for wild milk.

Sometimes one must die for the other to live. Then the survivor must spend the rest of his life trying to outrun his brother's ghost. Even death is not an end, not a true victory. The one who survives will always be haunted.

No one can ever bury his own shadow.

When you look into the night sky, the stars you see are billions of years old. It takes that long for their light to reach you. By then, the star could already be dead. What you are seeing is only a memory.

All stars die eventually. If it is big enough, it will collapse into itself and form a black hole. It will suck in everything around it. The bigger a star gets, the messier its downfall, the more it takes down with it.

But before that, it will explode in a supernova. Before it retreats into the graveyard of the universe, it will light up the sky in one last gasp of beautiful violence.

I wake up to Lulu licking my face. Artemis is standing on my belly, her tiny hooves like drills into my ribs. Her head is cocked to the side, looking at me as if asking what I'm doing here. "Good morning," I say. Artemis baas her welcome.

I vaguely remember waking up in the middle of the night, sore and twisted in Dylan's narrow bed. I remember the sour smell of his sleeping breath and my acute need to come here. I remember climbing into Lulu's pen, lying in the opposite corner to where Artemis and Penelope were curled up beside their mother, their tiny eyelids closed in the perfect sleep of babies.

I taste the residue of last night in my mouth. My head hurts and feels fuzzy, and my back is sore from sleeping on the ground. But mostly I feel tired and kind of sad, like my brain and heart just ran a marathon and now they need a day off. All I want is to be in a bed—a *real* bed, not my cot in the half-built yurt. I want four solid walls and a roof over my head. I want to eat the meat of an animal whose name I don't know.

It is dark in the barn. The sun is low in the sky, barely risen. On a normal day, I might be getting here soon to collect the eggs for breakfast and let the animals out of their pens. But today has been declared a holiday on the farm so everyone can sleep off the madness of last night.

Except for Doff. I hear the clanking of the barn doors as he pulls them open; I watch everything brighten as he lets the morning in. He never has the day off. The vegetables can wait for everyone else to recover, but Doff has all these animals counting on him. He is responsible for lives other than his own.

He opens the gate to the goats' pen and does not seem surprised to see me lying in the corner. Lulu and Penelope run over to greet him, but Artemis stays put on my lap, loyal to me.

"Crazy night last night?" Doff says, smiling.

"Kind of."

"Didn't see you there much."

"I left early." He opens the door to the field, and all three goats run out into the day. Without them in the pen with me, I suddenly feel the ridiculousness of my location. I stand up too quickly, and the barn whooshes around me. "Did you have fun?" I say, trying to cover up my dizziness. "At the party?"

"It was okay." He doesn't elaborate. I can read his silence; I can sense the absence of Lark. There is a hole in his evening where she should have been.

"Let me help," I say, "with the animals today."

"No way, kiddo," he says, trying to mask the sadness in his voice. "You have the day off."

"It's okay," I say. "I don't mind."

"Nope," he says. "I'm putting my foot down. Go have some fun. It's an order."

Have some fun? Doesn't he realize how much harder that is than it sounds?

I leave him at the barn and walk toward the camp. I don't know what I expect to find there—people strewn about in various stages of undress, upended tables and broken chairs, buildings half burnt to the ground. But all that's there is a smoldering pile of embers where the bonfire was. Dishes have been washed, chairs have been returned to their tables, and drums have been put away.

The patio is quiet and surprisingly peaceful. A handful of children eat breakfast with bedraggled-looking parents. The majority of adults are probably still sleeping. Maybe I can grab a quick breakfast without anyone talking to me. Maybe I can sneak away and find a quiet place by the lake and make myself invisible for the day.

But when I walk into the kitchen to find food, I quickly realize that is not what's going to happen. There is Sadie with Lark and Skyler, drinking coffee and chatting. She's pale and skinny from her weeks in quarantine, but her eyes are full of fire. Just like that, she's the star again, like she was conjured out of the bonfire by last night's ritual.

"Max!" she cries when she sees me. She runs over and throws her arms around me. "I'm back!"

"Yay," I say, but it sounds like a lie as soon as it comes out of my mouth, like she squeezed it out of me with her hug, like I'm one of those dolls that's programmed to say things little girls want to hear.

Sadie looks at me, her eyes wide and already hungry. "Mom told me about the party last night, so don't bother trying to hide it from me," she says, and I feel a moment of panic, like my feet aren't touching the ground, like I'm about to be thrown against the wall by some force outside my control. But then Lark and Sadie laugh. "Oh, Max," Sadie says.

"I wish I could have been there. It sounds like it was quite a show."

"I left early," I say, still not sure I'm off the hook.

"I figured," Sadie says. "Mom said it was pretty nuts."

"There's a lot I love about this place," Lark says, then leans in and whispers conspiratorially, "but they can go a little overboard sometimes with the woo-woo shit."

Lark and Sadie laugh, and I feel a little sorry for the people who took last night so seriously, who really believed they were doing magic. Skyler looks confused, like she doesn't understand what they're laughing at. This is the only world she's ever known. This is the only thing she's ever been taught to believe in. "What's so funny?" she says, and I feel a twinge of sympathy for her.

"Oh, nothing," Lark says. Then, "I'm just so happy my little girl is finally feeling better." She puts her arm around Sadie and gives her a squeeze.

"Me too," Skyler says, and throws her skinny arms around them.

They all look at me, like they're waiting for me to join their pile of love. "Me three," I finally say, but I cannot bring myself to take part in the group hug. I have a brief flashback of last night, that sudden feeling of freedom and clarity, of being unbound and unafraid. And now I can feel it slowly slipping away. Maybe it was just a hallucination. Maybe nothing ever really changed. Maybe everything's the same as it was before Sadie got sick.

"What should we do today?" Skyler says.

Sadie's eyes sparkle. "We should definitely start with some swimming," she says, ready to reclaim the lake as hers.

Sadie says she feels better than ever. She wants to go to town, wants to party, wants to do anything besides sit around while everybody works. The doctor said she still shouldn't do any physical labor for a couple weeks, even though I've never seen her so energized. She's like one of those hyperactive little dogs that pulls so hard at its leash it chokes, then as soon as it's released it rockets into space like a slingshot, a blur of fur and high-pitched yapping. It runs around, sniffing everything, jumping up on everyone it sees, shaking with pent-up energy, ready to explode. I told Sadie yesterday that she reminded me of a Chihuahua, and she got so mad she said she'd never speak to me again. The silent treatment lasted fifteen minutes, which is a long time for someone who usually needs to fill up every silence she finds.

I am spending more time at the barn than I have to. I stay late, cleaning things I've already cleaned. Doff doesn't say anything, just pats me on the shoulder when he leaves and says I'm doing a good job. I think he understands why I've been stalling, why I've been making up chores for myself. It's not only me who prefers the company of animals to people.

This is the only place I can really relax anymore. When I'm back at camp, I'm always nervous I'm going to run into Sadie, Lark, Skyler, and even Dylan. I haven't seen him at all since the night of the bonfire, haven't walked by him lounging on the porch of his cabin drinking beer in the afternoon, haven't passed him on his way to do one of his mysterious chores. It's like he disappeared into thin air again and took his truck with him. I have a vague memory of feeling a new connection to him, but with him gone I'm afraid it's quickly dissolving. Part of me is afraid to see him, afraid to find out that our connection was only a hallucination.

But I barely have time to miss him, now that Sadie's healthy and bored and on the prowl for entertainment. She always seems to find me within minutes of my stepping foot in the main house, like she's hiding in the shadows getting ready to pounce. Skyler is always close behind, ready to laugh at every joke Sadie tells, ready to *ooh* and *ahh* at every one of her stories, but I've heard them all already.

And so I hide. I pretend my life exists only in the confines of this barn and the fenced-in fields around it. So far, it's been working. So far, this is a place Sadie hasn't bothered to visit.

"Max!" a voice yells from the barn doors.

Until now.

I look to the doors and see her black silhouette outlined by sunlight. I see the smaller cutout of Skyler behind her. "Hi," I say, not bothering to yell.

"Damn, this place stinks!" Sadie announces. As she gets closer, her features solidify. She has spent her first few days of freedom soaking up the sun, making up for lost time. Her skin is tanned, giving her a healthy glow. Skyler is red-nosed and burnt beside her, freckles like mud splatter on her cheeks.

"How can you stand it in here?" Sadie says. "It smells like shit."

"Literally," Skyler says.

"You get used to it," I grunt as I shovel a load of manure and dirty straw into a wheelbarrow.

"Oh my God, Max. You are so butch!" Sadie laughs.

"These guys are cute," Skyler mews from the goat pen, where she is sticking her head over the fence. I feel a surge of protectiveness. I don't want anyone near my babies, especially not them.

"Come here, Sadie!" Skyler says. "You have to see this."

Sadie peers into the pen. "What are those?"

"Baby goats," I say. "They're only a couple weeks old. I helped deliver them." I can't help but feel proud, even superior. I have done something amazing that Sadie has never done.

"What do you mean, you helped deliver them?"

"I mean, I was here when the mother gave birth. I helped pull them out. I wasn't even wearing gloves." I don't know why I expect her to be impressed by this, but I guess I'm not surprised when she looks at me in horror.

"Max, that's disgusting."

"No, it's not," I say. Skyler is dangling a piece of straw into the pen, luring the babies with it, then pulling it away as soon as they get close. "Don't do that," I say, my voice rising.

"We're playing," she says.

"Those goats are so stupid," Sadie says.

"No, they're not!" I shout, pulsing with so much anger the barn seems to wobble around me. Sadie and Skyler both look at me like I'm crazy. I wish the barn had locks to keep them out, I wish it were hidden, I wish they had never found me here. They have ruined it by just breathing; they have poisoned the air with their words.

"What's wrong with her?" Skyler asks Sadie, like I'm not even here. I think for a second how satisfying it would be to throw this shovelful of manure at them.

"Yeah, Max," Sadie says. "What's wrong with you?"

"What's wrong with *me*? You walk in here and start insulting my work and expect me to not be pissed? And you're just walking around like this is a fucking resort, like you're on vacation, with your little troll following you around. What's wrong with *you*, Sadie?"

Skyler's face falls, and I immediately feel bad for bringing her into it. But I wanted to hurt Sadie, and I feel a sick satisfaction at her shocked expression. She doesn't say anything for a long time, just stands there with her mouth open while Skyler slowly backs away, then turns and walks out of the barn.

"Say something," I demand.

Sadie closes her mouth.

"Sadie, say something!"

"I'm sorry," she finally says.

"Sorry for what?" I want her to list off every single way she's ever hurt me, every thing I've had to do for her, every time I've held her hair while she puked, every time I've had to lie for her, apologize for her, every time I've been terrified because of something she's done, every time I've been ashamed and hurt and sad and lost. I want her to apologize for getting sick and leaving me. I want her to apologize for getting better and coming back. I want her to apologize for all the pain I've ever felt, because in this moment it feels like she's the cause of all of it.

"I'm sorry," she says again. "I didn't mean to hurt your feelings. I was just joking."

I search her face, but I'm not sure what for. Maybe I want to see some kind of recognition of what she's guilty of, some acknowledgement of blame. But I see nothing. We catch each other's eye for a second, and it feels like one of those awkward moments when you make eye contact with a stranger on the street—except this is supposed to be my best friend. I have spent my whole life watching her and learning her cues, but now we have exchanged places. She's trying to figure *me* out. Attention has shifted. The gaze has been reversed, and neither of us knows what we're looking at.

It is me who looks away first. I shovel another load into the wheelbarrow. I focus on the movement so I don't have to think or feel.

"Dylan's back, you know," Sadie says, breaking the silence. For a moment, I think she knows about us, and I feel a surge of panic. I am not supposed to have secrets. I am not supposed to take the boy she wants. But then I realize she was just looking for something to say, something to change the subject, something neutral that has nothing to do with us.

I don't say anything. I don't want her to get off so easily. I want her to suffer.

"Max, come on," she pleads. "I'm sorry. I'm really, really sorry. I was an asshole."

"Yes, you were," I agree.

"You're my best friend, Max. I miss you. Forgive me?"

"I'll think about it," I say. It is comforting to see her grovel.

"I love you," she says, coming close and wrapping her arms around me. She smells like clean hair, like flowery deodorant, like the absence of sweat.

"I love you too," I say, relaxing a little, hugging her back, hoping I get a little of my stink on her.

"Oh," she says, perking up. "Like I was saying. Dylan got back late last night." She pauses for dramatic tension. "And he has a *black eye*." She's grinning proudly at the delivery of this news.

"What? A black eye?" I say, not even trying to hide my shock. "How? From who?"

"How should I know? It's not like he talks to me."

I think about our wild night in the cornfields, Dylan following me even though I was blind, how frail and lost he looked when I finally got my sight back.

"Let's go see him," Sadie says. "Right now." I know this tone in her voice. It is the sound of her wanting to get into trouble.

"I have work to do."

"It's quittin' time," Sadie says, pulling the shovel out of my hand and throwing it to the ground. "I'm kidnapping you. If Doff complains, blame it on me."

I sigh. I am too tired to fight anymore. "Can I take a shower first?"

"No," Sadie says, tugging me toward the barn doors. "No time."

"But I'm covered in shit, Sadie."

"That's what the lake's for."

We are walking so fast it doesn't hit me where we're headed until we're almost there. Dylan's cabin. As much as I've missed him, and as much as I've fantasized about his mouth and his hands since he's been gone, I don't want to see Dylan right now. I don't want him to see me in these baggy jeans Doff gave me, this stained men's T-shirt rolled up at the sleeves, this farmer's tan on my arms, this ratty ponytail pulled through the back of a baseball cap. I don't want him to see me like this next to Sadie, with her evenly tanned skin, her short dress just out of the laundry, her long bruise-free legs and arms, her perfect cleavage. Is she wearing makeup? Jesus, Sadie, who wears makeup on a farm?

He's there, on his porch, watching us from behind dark sunglasses. He makes no sign that he differentiates between us, that I am any less a stranger than Sadie, that we have shared each other's saliva and touched each other under our clothes, that I have slept in his bed. Sadie practically skips up to him, her hair bouncing like a shampoo commercial. The porch is already littered with beer bottles, and it's not even five o'clock.

"Hey, Dylan," Sadie says, leaning over the rail of his porch so her boobs get pushed up. I know she's doing it on purpose. I know what her mating dance looks like. And I am fully aware that every trace of femininity I once had is hiding somewhere far away. I watch Sadie grab the beer from Dylan's hand and chug the whole thing. I watch him hand her another one. I feel sick, like it was me who just chugged that whole beer, like its fermented froth is sloshing around in my stomach and making me woozy. I can't watch this.

"I'm going swimming," I yell loud enough for Sadie to hear. As she turns around to wave at me, Dylan lifts his sunglasses. His left eye and nose are bruised, but I can still see the smirk behind the swelling. Our eyes meet, and I am suddenly breathless, made dizzy by a sickening combination of anger and lust. They are both looking at me, Dylan and Sadie, and I have never felt so much repulsion and so much craving in my whole life.

"Why don't you join us?" Dylan shouts, saying so much behind his words that Sadie can't hear. He's saying I am still a warm body he wants to touch, but this is not something he wants to announce publicly.

I don't say anything. I can't open my mouth. So I walk away, past the deflated raft that's been stuck there since we got here so many weeks ago, past the lily pads hiding the muck lurking below. I hear Sadie's laughter in the breeze. The wind will carry her song across the fields. Men will hear its whisper for miles around and wonder why they are suddenly aroused. Let her claim her domain. What do I care? For the time being, she has forgotten that I exist, and I am free until she has news to report.

I try not to feel the snake of jealousy burning through my ribs. I tell myself I don't even want him; she can have him. But the logical thoughts of my mind are doing nothing to cool me down. I am not convinced. I want him. I want him to want me. I want him to want me more than he wants her. I want him to hurt her. I want her to run back to me, crying, needing me, with a broken heart only I can fix. I want to mean something to them. I want to be important. Necessary. I want the feeling I used to have with Sadie, with my mother, that feeling of knowing someone can't live without me.

But it's gone. All I have is this body, sticky with sweat and dirt and animal shit. I walk far away from everyone, behind a tall patch of reeds where the farm is hidden from view. I don't care that this part of the lake is murky and tangled with mysterious weeds, I don't care that no one can see me, that I could be pulled under and disappear and no one would notice until it was too late. I throw off my clothes and step into the water, completely naked. I feel it wash over me like a baptism, even though there is no one here to bless me. I sink my head under and look up at the sky. The darkness swirls around me like a tunnel, and the sun shines at the end of it like a distant star, and I can't decide whether the light is a taunt or a promise.

After some persuading, I let Sadie fish me out of the water. She drags me to my yurt, picks out clothes for me to wear, the whole time repeating a chant of "What's wrong?" and "Are you still mad at me?" I don't like seeing her this way, all pathetic and unsure. I don't know which Sadie is worse— the one who takes me for granted or the one who needs me too much.

"Why are you being so quiet?" she keeps saying. "What are you thinking about?" I have nothing to say to that. I'm not going to tell her I secretly wish she'd get sick again so I can have my life back.

At dinner, she doesn't protest when I say I want to sit with Maria and Joseph. "So nice to finally spend some time with you," Maria says, little Bean attached to her breast as usual. "I'm so glad you're feeling better."

"Thanks," Sadie says, and I can tell she's trying hard to not stare at Maria's boobs.

"So, tell us about yourself, Sadie," Joseph says. "What kind of stuff are you into back in Seattle?"

I realize I'm nervous. I'm holding my breath, waiting for her to answer. I don't quite trust Sadie around my new friends.

"Well," Sadie says. "I like to go to shows." She doesn't mention how this is secondary to drinking.

"What kind of shows?" Maria asks.

"Oh, you know. Music. There's a lot of local bands in the Northwest."

"Joseph used to be in a band," Maria says as she switches Bean to her other breast.

"Really?" I say. "What kind of band?"

He chuckles. "It was in college. We weren't very good. Basically we were a mediocre jam band trying to be Phish."

Sadie snorts, then covers her mouth with her hand and looks at me apologetically. I resist the urge to pinch her leg under the table. But Joseph is so good-natured, he laughs it off. "I know," he says. "Probably not the coolest music, right?"

Before Sadie has a chance to attempt an answer, Maria says, "Do you know what your plans are for after high school?"

"Not really," Sadie says, pushing the food around on her plate.

"Max was telling us she's thinking of going to school to be a veterinarian," Maria says.

Sadie looks at me, shocked. "You didn't tell me that."

"It was something I was thinking about," I say, wanting to run from the table. "It's not for sure. It was just an idea."

I wait for her to cry, to stomp away in anger. But she smiles a little sadly and says, "It's a good idea, Max. You'd be good at that." For some reason, this makes my heart jump in my throat, makes the hint of tears surface in my eyes.

"Thanks," I say quietly, so only she can hear.

After dinner, people congregate in the living room to play charades. "Really?" Sadie whispers in my ear with her cynical hiss.

"I want to play," I tell her, and she looks shocked, then confused, then pleading.

"Come on, Max," she whines. "Let's steal a bottle of wine and go hang out by the lake, just the two of us."

"I want to hang out here."

She gets too close, whispers conspiratorially in my ear. "But these people are so weird."

I step back, look her in the eye. "I like them," I say. "They're good people, Sadie."

I see her jaw clench. I can tell she's trying so hard to not say something mean, trying to be agreeable, trying to give me what I need. Part of me is grateful; in some ways, I think this is what I've always wanted from her—to just notice my needs, to just *try* to not be so selfish. But watching her squirm like this, seeing how uncomfortable it makes her to be nice—part of me wonders if this will ever be enough.

"Okay," she says, and attempts a weak smile.

We sit down to play and a woman named Eleanor sets out a few wine bottles and cups on the table. "My first attempt at mead," she says.

"What's that?" Sadie says.

"Honey wine."

"Thank God," Sadie says under her breath as she rushes over to get her sample.

Everyone else sips slowly at the thick, strong wine, but Sadie's already filled her glass twice by the time everyone's played a round of charades. It's kind of like drinking syrup, and I have no idea how she can down it so fast. By the time we've played two rounds, Sadie's already talking too loud and laughing at things that aren't funny. This is always when my heart starts beating fast, when my breathing shallows, when my eyes start darting around for signs that Sadie's outstayed her welcome.

"It's so funny," Sadie says to Yoshiro. "You're so tiny and your wife is so *big*." She is the only one laughing.

This is when I'd save the day, when I'd swoop in and save

her from herself. This is when I'd be on high alert for damage control, when I'd carry her home and spend the rest of the night watching her either puke or sleep. But I refuse to do that this time. I refuse to let her decide when my night is over.

"Sadie," I say quietly, trying to avoid embarrassing her. "I think you should leave."

"What?" she says, spinning around so fast she knocks over her drink. "Oh, shit!" She retrieves the cup from the ground, her first instinct not to clean up the mess but to suck the remaining drops of wine from the cup.

"Sadie," I say again. "You're drunk. I think you should go to bed."

"But I don't want to go to bed," she says too loudly. I can feel every eye in the room on us.

"Sadie, come on."

"Where's my mom?" she says, looking around. "Have you seen her?"

"Let's go, Sadie," Doff says, moving toward her from his quiet place in the corner. He lays his hand gently on her shoulder.

"Where is she, Doff?" Sadie says, allowing him to help her stand.

"Probably sleeping," he says, but I know he doesn't really think that.

Doff leads her toward the door, and I can see Sadie's eyes

already drooping. "That wine was strong," she says, and there are a few kind giggles around the room.

"Goodnight, Sadie," people say. She waves goodbye with a big grin on her face, like she's on a float in a parade. Maria and Joseph are both looking at me with such compassion in their eyes I can't stand it. I don't want them to see me, don't want them to acknowledge how this hurts. I don't want to hear what people say after Sadie is gone, don't want to hear their comments, all their judgments wrapped in kindness. So I get up too and I leave out the other side of the house, trying not to feel the burn of eyes on my back, trying not to hear Maria's sweet voice ask me where I'm going. I may not be taking Sadie home, but I'm still letting her ruin my night.

I can hear Sadie babbling to Doff as he helps her down the trail on the other side of the lake. Her voice bounces off the water and takes over the night. I walk my trail alone, with nothing to distract me from the voices shaming me in my head. How could I have thought Sadie was capable of changing? How could I have been so stupid? And then it hits me, like a boulder, like an avalanche, how incredibly lonely I am. I am in the dark in the middle of nowhere, and the only people I've ever known how to love are lost to me—Sadie, my mother, my father—all gone in their separate ways. What do I have left? Who?

I know I shouldn't go to him, but I want that feeling back, even if it was just a hallucination. I want Dylan the way he was that night in the field, fragile and yearning and needing me, when he was lost, when I was the one who knew the way. I want him the way he reached out for my hand, the way he trusted me to show him the way home.

I know he's on his porch before I see him. I can feel his energy in the air. "Hey," he calls from the shadows.

"Hey," I say back. I climb the steps to his porch. He is leaning against the wall with his legs out. I straddle his legs and pin his arms down. "Where were you?" I say, my lips so close to his I can feel him suck in air.

"Damn, girl," he says. He tries to lift his arm, but I put more weight on it. He laughs. "I wouldn't have thought you were into this kind of thing."

"Where'd you go?" I say. "After that night. Why'd you disappear?"

"It was work stuff," he says. "Deliveries. I didn't really have a choice."

"You didn't tell me you were leaving. You didn't say good-bye." I lean in harder. "Then this afternoon you acted like you don't even know me."

Then all of a sudden I am flipped over, on my back, my arms pinned down. Dylan's on top of me, his face dark in front of the moon, his thighs pressing hard against mine. I feel my heart pounding hard in my chest, the muscles tight in my arms, straining enough to feel caught, but not enough to get away.

"First of all," he says. "*You* left *me* first. Remember? I woke up the next morning and you were gone." I stop fighting. I arch my back. I lift my pelvis to meet his. "Second of all," he continues. "I know how girls get, and I could tell you two are in the middle of something I definitely don't want to be a part of. So it seemed like a good idea to keep my distance, okay? Avoid whatever's going on that's got your fangs out. Sound fair?"

"Yes," I say breathlessly. His hands are still on my wrists. I squirm a little under him, but not too much.

"Do you want me to kiss you?" he says.

"Yes," I say.

"Maybe I should make you beg." His face is hovering over mine.

"Fuck you," I say. He laughs as he presses his lips against mine. His tongue is thick in my mouth. He tastes like beer and whiskey, like cigarettes, and despite the heat, despite every part of my body wanting to grab on to him as hard as possible, I feel a momentary revulsion, like this is not at all what I wanted, not at all what I was yearning for. He tastes like something rotting. His body feels like a dead weight on top of me.

I push him off. I sit up. I gasp for breath, for the taste of clean air. I rub my wrists where he held them so tight.

"What happened?" he says, pulling himself up.

"Why do you drink so much?" I say.

"What?" he says. "What are you talking about?"

"You drink all day long," I say. "That's not normal."

"One minute you're frothing at the mouth you want me so bad, and the next minute you're criticizing my drinking? Girls are crazy." He pulls me onto his lap, wraps his arms around me, kisses my neck. I begin to melt. All thought disintegrates. His hand goes to my zipper. An alarm goes off in my head.

"I know practically nothing about you," I say, breaking out of his arms. "Why is that?"

"Jesus, what's with all these questions?" I can tell he is losing patience.

"I want to know you."

"Why?"

"Because that's what people do in a relationship."

He laughs, and I feel the slice through my heart before he even says it. "Who said this was a relationship?"

I turn to stone. Stones don't breathe. Their hearts don't beat. Stones don't feel anything.

"Oh, fuck," he says. "Come on, calm down." I feel him pawing at me. "This is fun, right? That's what we're doing—

having fun. That came out wrong. I'm sorry, okay?"

He starts kissing me again, but my lips don't move. He wraps me up, pulls me tight to him, presses his face against mine so hard our teeth scrape. I try to pull away, but he's holding on too tight. This isn't fun anymore. This isn't a sexy game.

"What the fuck!" a voice says, tearing the night apart, tearing Dylan away from me. We both turn our heads to find Sadie outlined against the moon, her hair crazed and tangled and ominous. "What the fuck, Max?" she says, her voice a throaty mix of hurt and anger.

"Sadie," I say, but I can think of nothing more.

"Really?" she says. "This is happening? This is really happening?" She is shaking her head side to side, as if disagreeing with herself will make this less real. She is crying. The moonlight illuminates the tears running down her face. "Max, why didn't you tell me?"

Dylan slithers away into his cabin and shuts the door. "Fucking chicks," I hear him mutter.

Sadie backs away. "Wait," I say. "I can explain." But can I?

"Get off my fucking porch!" Dylan shouts from inside. "Take your little bitch fight somewhere else."

Sadie stumbles off the porch and starts running. "Sadie, wait!" I call after her, but she doesn't stop. She makes it halfway around the lake before she trips and falls to a heap on the ground. I jog up to her sobbing, slumped-over figure. She can't catch her breath. She's hyperventilating.

I rub her back. "Breathe, Sadie." She just looks at me with panicked eyes. "Look at me, Sadie. Listen to my breath." I breathe in slowly, out slowly. I grab her hand and place it on my chest. "In," I say. "Out."

It takes a while, but eventually she starts breathing normally again. And then she just cries. I hold her as she sobs. I whisper "I'm sorry" and "I should have told you" and "It's over now, anyway." I say these things over and over until she stops crying, until she's just limp in my arms.

"I was coming over to apologize," she says. "That wine was so strong, and my tolerance is so low now. I threw up when I got back to the trailer, and then I kind of sobered up." She looks up at me with so much love in her eyes, so much need, and just like that, so quickly, I forget why I've been so mad at her. All I remember is loving her. All I remember is needing her to love me.

"I'm sorry," she says. "I'm sorry I embarrassed you."

"I'm sorry I didn't tell you about Dylan. It just sort of happened." I smooth her hair down with my hand. "I think I was afraid you'd be jealous."

"I *am* jealous," she says, attempting a laugh, but it just comes out like an exhausted sigh. "Of a lot of things."

"What could you possibly be jealous of me for?"

"How happy you seem these days. How well you're fitting in here. How easy you make everything look."

"It hasn't been easy," I say.

Sadie sits up, puts her arms around me, and squeezes tight. "I miss you, Max."

"I miss you too," I say, and squeeze back. I miss our old ease. I miss having a partner. I miss not feeling so alone.

"Stay here with me," Sadie says when we get back to the trailer. I am tired, and the other side of the lake suddenly feels so far away. It is way too close to Dylan. So I climb into the twin bed and let her curl around me. I lie still, held captive by her long arms, listening to her peaceful breaths, wondering why it has always been so easy for her to fall asleep.

The air feels strange today. Heavy. Wet. Full of electricity. It was hotter than it should have been when I woke for my early shift at the barn, the air already soupy and oppressive even though the sun wouldn't rise for another hour. The animals were acting strange, skittish, more vocal than usual. In the rest of the world, they might call this earthquake weather. But the earth never moves here.

At breakfast, Sadie asks where I was this morning. I try to explain how I work early, how Doff and I trade mornings to wake up before dawn to collect eggs and let the animals out. She looks at me like I'm speaking a different language.

"I've been up for almost three hours already," I tell her. She blinks and takes a bite of toast.

"So, are you going to move back in or what?" she says.

"Oh," I mumble. "Uh." I hadn't even considered it.

"Just spit it out."

"I don't think so," I say. My chest tightens.

"That's what I thought you were going to say," Sadie says, looking down.

"I kind of like having my own space. It's like my own apartment or something, you know?"

"And the location isn't bad," she mumbles into her coffee.

"What is that supposed to mean?"

"You know."

"What? Living next to Dylan? I'm done with him, Sadie. Really. You walked in on the very last kiss I'm ever going to give him."

She flinches a little, as if the thought of me kissing him disgusts her. "Why?" she says.

"I started to realize that the more I got to know him, the less I liked him. Believe me, he was much more attractive when he was just pretty and mysterious." This makes her laugh a little. "It was much easier to objectify him."

"Yeah," she says, smiling sadly. "It sucks when they become, like, real people."

"Totally."

She takes another bite of toast and a sip of coffee. It's so unlike her to be silent, to sit there not talking when I know she has something to say. Finally, she looks up and says, "So you don't want to move back in with me?"

I could just say yes. I could do what Sadie wants. I could avoid the conflict altogether.

But maybe I can't do that anymore.

"I'm on such a different schedule than you," I say. "You don't want me waking you up at 4:30 every other morning, do you? You don't want me telling you to be quiet because I go to bed so early. You'd hate living with me right now, trust me."

Sadie's eyes fill with tears. "I just miss you, Max," she says.

"I miss you too." I get up and walk around the table to sit next to her. I put my arms around her, feel her familiar shape so perfect against me, as if we used to be connected like this in some former life.

"What about Skyler?" I say. "I thought she was your new best buddy."

"Very funny," Sadie sniffles. I squeeze her and let go. She looks at me with a slight grin, a trace of warmth returning to her face. "Have you noticed she's started talking like me?"

"I tend to not listen when she speaks," I say.

"Yeah, me neither."

"That poor girl." We laugh a little, and it feels good even if it is a little mean.

"Can we hang out tonight?" Sadie says, resting her head on my shoulder.

"Just us?" I say. "No mini-me?"

"I'll tell Skyler to scram."

"She'll be heartbroken."

"She's young. She'll get over it."

Sadie wraps her arms around me and squeezes surprisingly hard for someone so hung over.

"I love you, Max."

"I love you too." In this moment, I feel all our thirteen years of friendship all at once, and it is so much bigger than the last few weeks.

The animals are weird all day, and the air never loses its heavy feel, but I feel lighter, even happy. I'm excited to hang out with Sadie tonight. I'm excited to have my best friend back. Doff says a storm is coming, so we make sure to secure everything in case of strong winds.

"You're humming," Doff says as I'm tying up some rope.

"I am?"

"Yep. You're even smiling."

"Uh oh, I better stop."

He chuckles softly, but it's enough to rouse Che and Biafra from their naps on the floor. They lift their heads and wag their tails, looking at Doff expectantly, as if hoping for more laughter. "You and Sadie must have made up," Doff says.

"How'd you know we were fighting?"

He smiles and shrugs. He goes back to stacking tools.

I work fast so I get done with my chores early. I'm looking forward to showering, then meeting Sadie by the lake so I can work on getting rid of this farmer's tan.

But right as I am thinking this, I see him, just past some bushes, on a trail that leads to a part of the farm I never go. He is talking with Old Glen, far enough away that I can't hear what they're saying. I have the immediate impression that they don't want to be seen, so I hide behind a tree and watch.

Old Glen's face is twisted in anger, his shoulders leaning forward, like those of an animal getting ready to fight. I can't make out the words, but I can hear enough to know he's yelling, his voice like violent jabs in the air. Dylan throws his hands up in surrender, his eyebrows arched in apology. I can read the words on his lips: "Sorry, man," over and over, while Old Glen lays into him. Then Old Glen shoves him, pushing Dylan into the spikes of a blackberry bush. Dylan doesn't fight back, just hides his face with his hands, suddenly a little kid, waiting for it to be over.

Old Glen steps back, drops his hands, lets out a big sigh, and shakes his head. He's talking softly now, trying a new tactic of persuasion. Dylan looks up sheepishly, nods a few times, then Old Glen smiles and slaps him on the back like they're old pals, like nothing happened.

I can't watch any more. It seems like everywhere I turn, there is some new revelation that leaves me disgusted. With Dylan, with this place, with myself. I want to take a shower. I want to be clean and lie on a blanket with my best friend and talk about meaningless crap. Is that too much to ask?

I try to avoid people on my way to the shower. I go around the back of the house instead of through it or by the patio. But I run into Lark, and she tells me my dad called and wants me to call him back. Of course everyone I don't want to talk to suddenly wants to talk to me.

There is nothing better than getting clean after you've been covered in sweat and dirt and shit for eight hours. My shower is miraculous. I feel the day wash off me, and I start feeling hopeful again. Sadie said she'd go to town today and pick up some magazines and nail polish for our afternoon by the lake, and I can't think of anything I'd rather do than paint my toenails and make fun of celebrities.

But when I step out of the shower, there he is. I did not hear him come in, but here is Dylan, standing in front of me with his shirt off. The bruise on his face has lightened and turned yellow around the edges. His forearms are scratched and bleeding from his fall into the blackberry bushes. His hair is a mess, and he hasn't shaven in days. Seeing him like this, it's hard to remember what I found so sexy about him.

"Hi," he says.

"Hi." I am wearing only a towel. The room is too hot, too humid. "I was just leaving."

"Stay," he says.

I pretend not to hear him. "I saw you and Old Glen fighting."

"So," he says, coming closer.

"Is that who you got the black eye from?"

"That old fart? Are you kidding me?"

"Then from who?"

"You mean 'whom'?"

"Fuck you," I say.

He grabs me by the shoulders and pulls me to him. "If you insist," he says.

I taste the beer on his breath. I feel his hands, hot and forceful. I feel the air heavy around us, pushing us closer. A familiar feeling returns, the dizzying combination of anger and desire, and I realize there is only a very fine line between caressing and scratching, between kissing and biting.

His hand finds its way under my towel, between my legs. Our breathing sounds like animals panting. I could just let go. I could let him do whatever he wants with me. It's not like I wouldn't enjoy it. Is that what really matters in the end? Is pleasure the ultimate goal? Do things like love and respect and whether or not you even like someone just get in the way?

No. I refuse to believe that. My body cannot make my decisions. My body does not consider how I'd feel afterward, how I'd feel during, how I'd feel knowing the person touching it doesn't care about anything besides my skin, that I don't care about anything besides his.

"Stop," I say.

I feel the smile in his kiss. He thinks I am kidding. He pushes me against the steamy wall. I feel the slime of mildew on my back. He kisses me harder. He thinks my resistance is a game.

"I mean it," I say. I push him away. He looks at me, unbelieving.

"Are you fucking kidding me?"

"No," I say. "I'm serious."

He laughs. He laughs like I am the biggest fool he's ever seen. "You fucking coward," he says. "You little bitch."

His words shatter me. I open my mouth to speak, but nothing comes out.

"You think you're so good you're worth saving?" he snarls. "No one's that good." He stumbles out, shirtless, leaving me shivering, cold for the first time in weeks.

I focus on my breath. I breathe until I stop shaking. My mind is blank but my whole body feels like lead, like my veins are full of it, like I weigh a million pounds. I dress in slow motion, feeling every millimeter of movement. The only thought I'll allow into my head is the promise to Sadie that I'd go swimming with her this afternoon. We made a date, and I can't break it. When I am dressed, I take a deep breath. I do my best to relax my face, to erase the fear and hurt Dylan stamped on it. I walk into the sunlight. I see thick gray clouds far off in the distance. The bugs are buzzing louder than usual.

As soon as I meet Sadie on her side of the lake, she notices something wrong. I don't want to tell her. I don't want to complicate our fragile peace. "Let's get in the water," I say before she has a chance to say anything. I can tell I am on the verge of tears. But if I cry, the lake will hide it.

I swim hard and long, until all I can feel is the burning in my lungs and arms and legs. I feel pleasantly exhausted as we float on our backs, and I think this may be the end of the pain for a while. Maybe if I keep myself as physically busy as possible, I won't have the energy to feel anything else.

But Sadie's not that easily tricked. As soon as we get comfortable on the blanket, she says, "Something's up with you. I can tell."

I have to tell her something, so I tell her about seeing

Dylan and Old Glen fighting. I pretend it shook me up. I think it is something safe to talk about, something that has absolutely nothing to do with me.

"Oh, that's all?" She laughs. "Max, you're so cute."

Fuck you too, Sadie.

"They're growing weed, you know," she says. "They were probably fighting about that."

"What?" I say. She announces this all so coolly, as if it's not even news.

"That's what they're doing all the time, where Dylan goes off to. That's what his job is here. He's the salesman."

"How do you know this?"

"He told me."

"When?"

"I don't know," Sadie says. "Sometime the other day?"

I am numb. I have no more room for feelings.

"So that's how he got his black eye?" I say slowly. "In some drug deal?"

"Probably," Sadie says, flipping through a magazine. "I don't know. He wouldn't tell me about that."

"I can't believe it."

"Why not? Have you taken a good look at these people?"

"I thought they just grew vegetables." As soon as I say it, I know how stupid I sound.

"You really think they could support three dozen people with a few acres of vegetables?"

"Where do they grow it?"

"You know that big gray shed out past the east pasture? The one that's almost as big as the barn, with all the solar panels on top? In there."

"Inside? Like with grow lights?"

"Yeah."

For some reason, this bothers me more than the fact that they're growing drugs—that they're doing it unnaturally, with artificial lights. "But this is a *farm*," I say.

"Max, you don't really expect them to grow several thousands of dollars' worth of pot plants outside, do you?"

"I thought that was a tool shed."

"A tool shed with an electric fence and barbed wire?" Sadie laughs. "You're so naive, it's adorable."

"Stop saying that." I am angry. I am fuming.

"What?"

"That I'm adorable. That I'm cute."

"But you are. It's a compliment." She's confused. She doesn't understand why I'd find this offensive. I look at her sitting there, cross-legged in her bikini, her tiny belly squished into unflattering folds. She is relaxed and temporarily unconcerned with her bad posture and ugly sun hat. In this moment, she is mine. Maybe she can't read my mind. Maybe she doesn't know me perfectly. But Sadie loves me, and right now, that is the only thing I have.

So I distract myself with magazines. We find out what fashions women are supposed to be wearing this season, what stupid things beautiful people are saying, what new diet is going to make us lose ten pounds in three days, what's happening in Hollywood. Somewhere between here and there is the real world, the place we used to live, but I am quickly forgetting what it looks like.

Πανδώρα

PANDORA

Prometheus was punished for being too kind. He did not steal fire from the gods; he simply retrieved it. He was the celestial Robin Hood, returning something useful to the poor people who needed it. But Zeus had no tolerance for the destitute, no tolerance for handouts. So he created women to punish mankind for their hero's socialist leanings.

And so she was born, the first woman, molded out of water and earth. Beauty was her lure, and evil was her dowry. Such was the legacy of women.

And just like Eve, she was curious, not a becoming trait for a woman. What hubris it was to think for herself, to wonder, to do contrary to what she was told; what a crime to want to know what was in that famous box. In a moment of defiance, she opened it, releasing all the evil into the world. It spilled over the land like storm clouds; it darkened the sky black. The acrid smoke seeped into every pore of every soul, infecting mankind with a filth that could never be washed off.

This is what made her famous: her illicit box; that dirty, forbidden thing.

But no one ever talks about what was at the bottom of the box, hidden under layers upon layers of future suffering. With the storm clouds thrashing in the sky grabbing all the attention, no one noticed the tiny pearl of light that remained at the bottom, the little crumb of hope like a lonely afterthought.

But shame is stronger than hope, and of course the first woman invented that, too.

"They're saying it's going to be a tornado," Old Glen announces calmly at dinner, which we're eating inside the cramped living room because the wind is blowing so hard outside. The room starts chattering. Adults comfort worried children.

"Ooh, a tornado!" Sadie says excitedly, as if he just announced her favorite band was coming to town.

Old Glen goes over the instructions for what everyone needs to do to prepare: take down the solar panels; tie down everything you can; come back to the main house as soon as possible; and whatever you do, don't stay in the yurts, trailers, and cabins, because they'll be the first thing a twister picks up. The adults nod knowingly. Doff and I make eye contact, and

I know he will stay with the animals through the storm. His smile tells me not to worry.

Lark flits by and puts her arms around us. "Don't worry, girls," she says. "Everything's going to be fine. This is totally normal. Happens a couple times every summer." Somehow I'm not convinced.

As everyone leaves to get ready, Lark squeezes my shoulder. "Your dad called again," she says. "He says it's important. You might want to call him before the phone lines go down."

"You go check on the trailer while I call my dad," I tell Sadie. "Make sure everything's secure." This is what I'm good at—telling her what to do in an emergency. She nods and slumps out the door with all the others who are running to outsmart a tornado.

The house is empty and silent, but I can see everyone running around outside, like a movie with the sound turned off. I sit in the corner where the phone is and call my house. I hold my breath, praying no one will pick up. I'm more scared of this phone call than I am of the tornado.

Dad answers on the first ring. "Hello?" he says. His voice sounds desperate. I don't know why, but I have a feeling he's been sitting by the phone in the kitchen all day, staring at it, waiting for it to ring.

"Dad?" I say. "It's me."

"Oh, Max," he says, sounding relieved. "I'm so glad it's you."

"Who else would it be?"

"Oh," he says. "Well."

"Dad, what is it? What's so important?" I decide not to tell him about the tornado. I don't want to make this conversation any longer than it has to be.

He doesn't say anything for a while. I can hear the phone line crackling, like the wind of the storm is blowing through the wires.

"Dad?" The wind is picking up, blowing bigger things around outside. A plastic chair clatters across the deck. Small waves lap at the shore of the lake.

"Your mom," he says, and everything stops for a moment. The wind stops blowing, people freeze midstride, birds float still in the air. I suddenly have no legs. I can't feel anything past my rib cage. The bottom half of me has been sucked into the earth, and I can feel it falling even though the rest of me is sitting right here.

"What?" I say. I think I am whispering. "Dad, what happened?"

"She's in the hospital," he says, his voice cracking. "She had an accident. Too many pills." I can hear him breathing hard, trying to push the tears away. "The doctors said she had enough in her to kill a large man twice over. But her tolerance was so high. That's what saved her. She's been taking so much."

Silence. We are waiting for each other to speak.

"She was dead, Max," he whispers. "Her heart stopped."

"Oh, God," I say. "Oh, God."

"They revived her. She's in the ICU. She—"

"Dad?"

I hear him stifle a cry.

"Dad!"

"She hasn't woken up yet."

"I don't understand." My body is disintegrating. I can barely feel the phone in my hand, against my ear. It is hanging there in the air, held up by phantom limbs.

"She overdosed, Maxie," he sobs, his voice blasting through the phone with so much force, it's like he'd been holding it in for years. "The police searched the bathroom and found pill bottles from seven different pharmacies. Oh God, Max." His heaving pushes air through the phone, his pain running through the lines from Seattle to Nebraska, reaching me, entering my skull. I see raindrops starting to fall outside. The wind throws them against the window like a million angry teardrops.

"It's going to be okay, right, Max?" He sounds desperate, crazed. "Right?"

"Why are you asking *me*?" I say, anger running through my veins like lava. "*You're* the dad. *You're* supposed to know the answers. Not me. I'm the kid. I'm the fucking kid, Dad." There is fire where my body once was, where numbness once was, fire replacing a ghost, destruction replacing the destroyed. I wish I were with him right now. I wish he were right in front of me so I could pound on his chest with my little kid fists.

"Max," he says, trying to sound strong. "I'm sorry. You're right. Everything's going to be okay. Mom's going to wake up and get the help she needs. We'll all help each other through this. Right, Maxie? Like a family. Right?"

"I don't know," I cry.

"It's going to be okay," he says, his voice so frail in its attempt to be firm.

"I don't believe you."

I can see him sitting on the stool at the kitchen counter, the sink full of dishes, a frozen pizza half eaten next to him, the rest of the house dark with our absence. I imagine him sleeping on the sofa with the TV on all night, rather than sleep in their bed alone with the silence.

"I have to go," I say, wiping my nose with the back of my hand.

"Max, are you okay? Are you going to be okay?" The half-eaten pizza has been sitting out for days. The cheese has turned to rubber. It is collecting flies.

"I don't know," I say, and I hang up, the feeling and sound of the receiver hitting the old-fashioned console so much more satisfying than just flipping off a cell phone could ever be.

I know it is cruel. I know I am hurting him. But I don't care. I don't care about anything. My mom could be a vegetable. A tornado is coming, and maybe it will take me. Maybe none of this will even matter in the end. I hear the phone ringing as I walk out of the living room. It took him a few seconds to find the number to call back. He had to search through the pile of unopened mail that has collected since I've been gone. I wonder what bills have gone unpaid. I wonder how he's managed to survive this long without me or her to take care of all the things women take care of.

I am done. I am done loving all of these broken people. I am done allowing them to keep breaking me. I am done caring so much, done trying to put them back together again, done hoping, done wondering why it never works out. It is not my job anymore. I quit.

The phone keeps ringing, but I walk out the door. The rain pounds, the sky thunders, and lightning flashes in the distance. People are running around, moving things inside, tying things down, taking the fragile solar panels off roofs. I head toward my yurt because I don't know where else to go, even though it's probably the least safe structure on the entire farm. I can't bear to be in the house with the ringing phone and the trails of my father's words.

Sadie and Dylan are sitting on Dylan's porch, drinking beers like none of this is happening. She is talking, but I can tell he's not listening. He's looking at me, a snarl on his lips. I should turn around. I should go back to the house, where it's safe. I should run away from this man who does nothing but make me feel like shit, away from this girl who does everything she's not supposed to.

"Max!" Sadie yells, waving her arms like she's worried I won't see her.

I should turn around, but I don't. There is no good place to go. There is only one path, and both directions lead to heartbreak. I approach Dylan's porch, but I do not look at him. Maybe it is possible to ignore his presence. Maybe I can just be with Sadie. Maybe I can sit so when I look at her, he will be on the other side, hidden. Maybe if I stare out at the lake, I can pretend nothing ever happened; Dylan never touched me, and I never touched him back.

"Max," Sadie says, her voice too loud. "I'm not scared. Are you?" How is it possible that she is already drunk?

"No. I'm not scared," I say, taking a seat beside her.

"Dylan says not to worry," she says. "It's only a tornado *watch*, not a tornado *warning*. They're totally different."

"Uh huh." I am looking straight ahead. I am like a horse with blinders. I see nothing beside me.

"And they give a tornado watch, like, every time it rains. Right, Dylan?"

"Something like that," he says.

"You're not mad at me?" Sadie says. "Because I didn't go secure the trailer like I was supposed to?"

"Give me a beer," I say. Sadie hands me a can of something cheap and I force myself to chug about half of it. I fight my gag reflex. I have always hated the taste of beer.

"God, Max," Sadie laughs.

"Is there anything stronger?" I say.

Sadie hands me Dylan's flask. "Are you okay?" she asks.

"I just want to catch up with you," I say. It's my turn to be reckless. It's my turn to not care. I pinch my nose and gulp down as much whiskey as I can until my throat catches on fire. I wash it down with the beer, still holding my breath. I beg my stomach to not send everything back up.

"Should we be doing something?" Sadie asks. The camp is like a giant stage in front of us, all the actors running around, the wind howling like a bad orchestra. We're sitting here in our box seats, spectators to everyone's fear.

"Nah," Dylan says, lighting a joint. He sucks in a big toke and passes it to Sadie. The herby sweetness of the smoke mixes with the electricity in the air.

"Wow, this is good," Sadie says, holding the smoke in, passing the joint back to Dylan.

"Hey," I say, grabbing it out of her hand. She looks at me, her eyes wide with surprise.

"But you don't smoke pot, Max," she says slowly.

"I do now," I say, taking a huge drag. I hear Dylan's cruel laugh coming from Sadie's other side. "What's so funny?" I cough.

"Nothing," he says. I drink the rest of my beer and grab a new one. I take a few more gulps of whiskey. It is spreading through my body, turning all my cells warm and numb. Maybe this is what I'm supposed to do. Maybe this is what letting go is supposed to feel like. I'm supposed to run away like Dylan and Sadie, make myself so drunk or high that I forget why I was upset in the first place. Run away from the phone, run away from my father's voice, run away from my mother and her pain, run and run until it all goes away, like it never even happened in the first place.

Sadie is clueless to the tension in the air. We pass the joint back and forth in silence. We watch Marshall drive from house to house collecting solar panels in the back of his truck.

Skyler and her mom join the others on their way to the house, carrying flashlights and lanterns, bags full of valuables. Skyler is clutching a stuffed blue bear to her little-girl chest.

"They're all so paranoid," Dylan says.

"What about your crop?" Sadie says with a conspiring voice, proud to be in on the secret.

"What about it?" Dylan says.

"Don't you have to go secure it or something?"

"It's taken care of."

"What do you mean?"

"Don't worry about it." The tone of his voice tells her this line of questioning is over.

But Sadie can't stay quiet for long. "What happens in a tornado?" she says, passing the joint back to me. I'm already way past the point when I usually stop drinking, when the buzz turns into something more serious, when I've always felt like I was starting to lose myself. But right now, I can't remember why I've always thought that was such a bad thing. Right now, that's all I want—to lose myself. I fill my lungs with smoke. I hold it until I'm sure it has seeped into every cell of my body.

"All this shit would be gone," Dylan says. "The fucker would pick up all these tents and trailers and throw 'em across the state. Trailer parks are the worst. If a tornado hits one of them, forget about it. Poor people are the first to go." Sadie laughs nervously.

"That's morbid," I say, despite my promise not to talk to him. For a moment, I forgot. For a moment, I thought we were just talking about tornadoes.

"Nature's morbid," he says. "Survival of the fittest. Only the strong survive."

"Are we going to get struck by lightning?" Sadie says.

"Only if you run around the fields holding a golf club in the air," Dylan says.

"A golf club!" Sadie cries hysterically. "Oh my God, what if we all went to my dad's golf club? Everyone here! What if we just showed up and said we wanted to golf there? They'd have to let us in, right? If they didn't, it'd be discrimination."

"You're wasted," I say, and I realize I am too. This is exactly the feeling I was looking for, like I'm someone else entirely. I've been turned into someone who doesn't care about anything. I don't care that I'm drunk and sitting outside on a rickety porch in a storm that might turn into a tornado. I don't care that my mom OD'd on prescription pills and might die. I don't care that I'm hanging out with a guy who called me a bitch two hours ago for not fucking him. I am done caring.

The joint has burnt down to a short, brown, wet nub. I hold it with the tips of my fingernails and suck like I've seen

Sadie and so many others do, all those countless times I stayed sober while everyone else got high, when I was so determined to stay in control, watching from the sidelines and resenting them all. I suck at it until I feel my fingers burning, and then I throw it into the rain.

"Let's go swimming!" I yell as I jump up. The porch buckles below me like it's made of Jell-o. I grab on to Sadie as I fall to the floor. I laugh as I try to prop myself up. Somehow my head lands in Dylan's lap. I look up at his face, and he's not so scary from down here. The lines separating his skin from the greenish-gray sky behind him are fuzzy. He sinks into the clouds, into the storm, just a piece of cruel weather.

Sadie pulls me off him, and we run toward the lake. We are throwing our clothes off. The rain is pouring so hard now, it's not even raindrops. We're running through a waterfall. I can't even tell when we reach the lake. It is water all over, water everywhere, from above and from below, sideways, diagonal, upside down. There is no difference between floating and flying.

Dylan is in the water too. We circle him like rabid mermaids. The sky starts falling in cold chunks the size of gravel, pieces of clouds made solid, splashing into the water.

"It's hailing!" Sadie screams, and she spins around with her hands out, trying to catch the balls of ice. The winds turn sinister, pounding us with the hard pellets, stinging us with the poison of a million frozen bees. The lake laps against us in tight waves, like hands pulling at our skin, hands trying to pull us under. The water is a whirlpool around me, below and above, water everywhere, spinning out of control. I reach out for Sadie for balance. She holds me by the elbows and yell-whispers into my ear, "You get his back and I'll get the front. Go. Now!" and I follow her through the sea in slow motion, fighting against the current trying to pull me away from shore. She parts the water and I follow. "Attack!" she says, and I do as commanded.

Then Dylan is the only one standing. We are curled around him, flexible as fish. He is holding us up. Sadie's mouth is on his, and I am only eyes, just watching. I am her mirror, and the sky is melting.

"I don't think this is a warning anymore," I say. I am spinning. I am corkscrewing into the sky. There is no land and no lake, it is just me and the rain and the sky and the tunnel, up and up and up into the heavens. I can't see. Only wet black in front of me. I hear a dark voice through the spinning: "You two. Kiss. Now." Then a laugh like from the bottom of a well, faraway and flimsy. Then lips on mine, unfamiliar, soft and hot and messy, a mouth tasting of beer and whiskey and pot and too much history. A foreign tongue darting in and out of my mouth, lost, flailing, like it knows it's not supposed to be there. We are wrapped inside the water, tangled. We become water. Then a faraway laugh. It is the laugh of someone who's won. It is the sound of being defeated.

I push and kick and I spit the tongue out. I am going down or up or sideways, as far as I can swim or run or fly, far away where no one can touch me. There are hands and then no hands, air and then no air. I am sucked into the lake or the rain, it doesn't matter which, just that I'm gone, away. There is no me left. Just a body full of water. Just a lake full of tears.

I kick and kick and go nowhere. It's impossible to fight water. It's impossible to win when you don't know which way is up. Fear and panic and kicking won't save me. I can't run when I'm held in place. I can't win if I'm the only one fighting, if what I'm fighting is water, if what I'm fighting is bigger and stronger than I will ever be, if it doesn't even bother fighting back, if it bends and dances around my thrashing, letting me think I'm doing something, holding me in place, holding up my war with myself, softening my screams with liquid silence. I can't breathe if I don't know which way is up, which way is air, with the weight of the world holding me down. But a vacuum must be filled, it is a law of the universe, emptiness cannot stay empty for long, the body wants to breathe even if the mind doesn't, it does it on its own, the lungs heave even if I'm screaming *No! No!* in my head. My mouth opens. The water enters. The cool wet relief. First. But then it burns. Then the water catches on fire in my throat, my lungs. I am burning with water. It is not water but gasoline. Someone lit a match. Fire. Fire. Fire inside. Fire everywhere.

But just as fast, the fire goes out. Water is stronger than fire. My lungs keep breathing this strange air like pudding. They are full. They got what they wanted. There is no vacuum. I am done. I am full.

The only thing left to do is let go. After all that struggle, all that fighting these impossible wars. Stop kicking and become water. Liquid. Soluble. Look up or down at what might be the surface, what might be the bottom, feel myself heavy, remember gravity, here it is. Here's my toe touching something squishy. I remember what down feels like. I am going there. I am going to the lake floor. I am gravity. I am going to rest with the things that sink down to decay and become fish food. I am letting go. I am breathing the syrup of death. Life blooms inside me like a showy flower going all out for its big finale.

So this is what peace feels like. This is what it means to stop fighting. This is darkness. This is my eyes closing. This is the end of the war.

There is silence here. Warmth in the darkness. Not like

the tunnel I found in the cornfields. Not like that hallucinated light. This is the real thing. Here I am. You can take me. I am ready to let go.

But first, flying. I am out of the water. I am weightless. I am watching forms turn into fish. Bodies entwined, eyes closed. They don't even know I am dead in the water just two feet away. They don't know there is another me flying up here, don't know I can see them kissing their pain away. They don't know how much they're not seeing, how closed their eyes, how lost in the storm.

My poor loves, I could never save you. I'm sorry I promised so many undeliverable things.

Voices. Barking. It is the hell dog Cerberus come to take me home. I am drowning in the river Styx. The hands of the dead grab at my feet, pulling for me to join them. People running, yelling words I can't hear. Water above and below. Desperate bodies torn apart. Someone covering you with a blanket. Doff punching Dylan in the face. Those peaceful hands so full of fear. Those calloused hands reaching into the water, pulling me out like a net full of fish. You screaming. You clawing your way to me. Someone holding you back, holding your arms in the blanket, shushing you like a baby. Dylan runs off into the night, into the storm, and no one cares. Goodbye, goodbye. I cannot remember his hot hands on my body. The taste of his mouth is nothing against this lake in my lungs.

Sadie, you are screaming unintelligibly. But I know what you're saying. I hear you from somewhere deep down—*I'm sorry I'm sorry*—it's all you can say. I wish I could wrap myself up with your shame and take it to death with me. I wish I could show you how to let go. But that was never my job. I know that now. *I'm sorry I'm sorry,* you keep screaming in this language of water only I can decipher. Oh Sadie, I know you're sorry. That was never the problem. I want to tell you, but you can't hear me. I want to tell everyone not to worry: Doff pulling me out with his strong arms, Lark holding you like her baby, everyone else surrounding the scene wanting to help, wanting to be useful, wanting to mean something, wanting to give something back to life.

Maria, take your baby inside. Don't stand here crying in the storm. Bean, it's going to be okay. I know that now. You can stop crying. You too, dogs, stop barking. There is nothing to be scared of. You're the only ones who can hear me. You're the only ones who can see me floating up here. Everyone else is too busy looking at that soggy old shell of me on the ground, the one Doff is trying to breathe life back into. Only the dogs and baby know where I really am. They look up while everyone looks down. I tell the dogs, "Sit," and they do. I tell the baby, "Shh," and he does. While everyone keeps screaming and crying, and the wind keeps howling, and the raindrops keep pounding out their pain.

And then, white. Not the light, but a hospital. Not warm, but sterile. Not now, but later. I am in the room, in the corner. Still floating. Still air. Still nothing except to dogs and babies. Mother, you are awake. You are in the bed and you are almost smiling. Dad, your hand is soft and strong around hers. I can feel how you're holding it, with just the right amount of pressure. Mom, you are tired. You have never felt so tired. I swim inside you and know how hard you had to fight to come back. But you did. You were at the bottom of the lake and made a decision. You got to the end of the tunnel and decided to turn around. Dad kisses you on the temple. There is only one thing missing. But I am already here! I can feel your heart breaking. The voice in your head—*I'm sorry I'm sorry.* Everyone is always so sorry. What if we all just stopped being sorry?

I know this is the tunnel. I know there are two ways to go. I know where the light is brighter. It calls me like a magnet, so warm, the warmest thing I have ever felt. It says stop fighting. It says let go. It says come here. Rest. Stop being sorry.

But there is another light at the other end. This one is smaller, covered up by so much mud. It's the light at the bottom of the box. It's the light that stayed when Pandora opened it, the one everyone forgets. We keep chasing the other one, the bright and flashy, the one that is so certain. But look at this beautiful thing hiding, this rare and precious thing, so small it's so often overlooked. There is hope shining in all these places I thought were dark, light hiding where I forgot to look, light like an afterthought, discarded by time, and I am its gleaner.

HADES, REVISITED

Ἅ¸δης

Here again, facing this lonely god.

You are as empty as we are, as yearning and lost. How can someone so sad be scary? Is loneliness what made you cruel, what makes you hoard these souls you have no real use for?

Your servant, Death—he is not cruel. He takes and takes, but like so many others who inflict pain, he is just doing his job—ruthless in his apathy, too broken to care. It is not hard to outsmart him. His heart is not in it. Some say he wants to be tricked.

I sneak out of your gloomy procession. That is not my blood on your altar. That is not my breath in your mouth. You have sent your servant too soon. You must wonder why my body's so light. I will tell you—it is only a shell.

Everyone must cross the water. They must put the coins on their eyes. They must sacrifice a lock of hair. These things can be measured. Grams and ounces.

But what is the weight of the soul? How many grams is defiance? How many ounces is light? Tell me, how do you measure hope?

Vague memories of choking, of breathing and not breathing, someone else breathing for me, someone else's breath in my lungs, pushing the lake out. Waking up, Doff hovering above me, concerned faces in the sky. Dogs barking, at war with the wind. Snapshots, then black. Life, then death, and then life again.

The lake took me, but then she spit me out. What I know is I'm alive. Doff pulled me out from the bottom of the lake and gave me his breath. His knuckles are bruised from giving Dylan a black eye to match his other. Sadie has been tucked into bed back at the trailer to sleep the night off. I am on a couch in the living room, naked and wrapped in quilts. Dylan and the green truck are long gone, escaped into the violent night.

It is morning. The sun shines bright through the window like it's in denial about what happened last night. It's a summer day like any other, despite the fallen tree limbs, upended chairs, and various loose items strewn about the farm. The funnel itself missed us by a couple miles, but the surrounding storm did some damage. Doff says we got lucky. Almost all of the structures stayed perfectly intact. Except my yurt. It was sucked into the night, leaving only the bare cracked skeleton of its frame. No one has found the rest of it yet, not to mention my stuff. Farmers for miles around will find my underwear hanging from ears of corn.

So now I am homeless. I have nothing. Luckily, I left my wallet in the main house, so at least I have identification, a flimsy piece of plastic that says I'm me. But I don't even have any clothes; I was naked when Doff found me, and the storm took everything I owned, sparing the rest of the farm for the most part, as if *I* was its target, as if God sent it just for me.

So now what? All I have is my name and a headache. All I have is a prepaid ticket back to Seattle, scheduled for a month and a half from now.

"How are you, sweetheart?" Lark coos, entering the living room with a pot of tea and some folded clothes I recognize as Sadie's. She pours me a cup and sets it on the coffee table along with the clothes. She sits on the edge of the couch and brushes the hair from my forehead. "How are you feeling?"

"Okay," I croak. My throat feels like sandpaper.

"You gave us quite a scare."

"Sorry," I say.

"Oh, Max, it's not your fault. I know it's not your fault." She looks out the window, her face sad. She has the same beautiful neck as Sadie, the same sharp jaw when her teeth are clenched.

"Whose fault is it?" I say, sitting up, suddenly full of energy, my hangover and near-drowning a distant memory. The residue of alcohol and lake has been replaced with fury. This is what it feels like to care. This is what it feels like to finally stop running. Sometimes it hurts. Sometimes it burns like breathing water. Somewhere in the back of my mind, I know Lark is not the source, but it is she who is in front of me right now, she who my rage is painting red.

She looks at me, a trace of fear or shame in her eyes. "He's gone," she says, already knowing it's not the right answer. "He's never coming back."

"Dylan?" I say. "It's not his fault. He's just an asshole who happened to be here."

We sit in silence for a while. Lark pours me a cup of tea, and I hold the mug in my hands, feeling its warmth, trying to draw it into the rest of my body to smooth out the tension.

I don't want to wear Sadie's clothes, don't want her hand-me-downs. Lark clears her throat, turns to me, and opens her mouth to speak. But she chickens out at the last minute, looking down at her hands and saying nothing. I look out the window at all the people cleaning things up, fishing their stuff out of the lake with brooms, hoisting the solar panels back onto their roofs, doing their work so efficiently, doing it because it needs to be done. If only life were that easy, with a simple set of tasks laid out in front of me, telling me exactly what to do, with none of this wondering, none of this ambiguity, none of this flailing around and drowning beneath the weight of it all.

Finally, after what seems like forever, Lark speaks. "You've been a good friend to Sadie," she says, still looking at her hands. "I don't know what she would have done without you all these years."

I don't know what to say. Thank you? Thank you for abandoning your crazy daughter when she was a baby and leaving me to take care of her?

"I've noticed things have been tense between you two lately," she continues. "I think Sadie really misses you. I think she's really hurting."

"Are you fucking kidding me?" is what comes out of my mouth. Lark looks as surprised as I am for saying it. But I can't stop. The storm unleashed something. I feel it raging through me. "You're trying to tell me about how *Sadie's* hurting? She's been sitting around all summer doing nothing while I've been working my ass off. She's been doing that her whole fucking life. Which, of course, you wouldn't know, because where have you been? And now you're trying to act all concerned like you actually give a shit? You say Sadie's missing me? You come to *me* to fix it? You think I'm responsible for what's going on between us?"

I want to hurt her. I want to hurt anyone. "Well, what's happening between you and Marshall?" I hiss. "I've seen you two together. I've seen you running off with him. I know what you're doing to Doff."

I am shaking. I am not breathing. There is no room for breath with all this anger. Lark's eyes fill with tears and shock, and I feel a cruel satisfaction in knowing I've hurt her. She buries her face in her hands and shakes her head back and forth slowly.

"Say something!" I demand. I pound my fist on the couch and a cloud of dust is its sad punctuation.

"Doff and I have an open relationship," she says into her hands. "He knows about Marshall."

"What does that even mean? An 'open relationship'? That's just an excuse for being slutty."

Lark looks up at me. "I know I've been a terrible mother," she says. "You think I don't know that? I knew from the beginning I'd be a terrible mother. That's why I left Sadie with her father. I knew it would be best for her."

"It didn't work," I snap. "She turned out just like you."

"I know," she whispers. "I'm sorry, Max. I'm trying to be a good mom now. I'm trying to make up for all that lost time."

"What, by spoiling her? By letting her get away with anything?"

"Maybe it looks like that to you," Lark says, reaching out to take my hand in hers. I shake it away and turn my head so I can't see the hurt in her face. "But I think what Sadie really needs right now is to know she's loved," she continues. "After all these years, I think that's what's really been lacking."

All the anger rushes out of me, pours out of my body and splashes on the floor. All that's left is an empty, aching hole. All that's left is the tiny yelp that comes out of my throat, the sound of all the air being shoved out of me.

"She's been loved," I say, and then I am crying. I am pushing everything out. I am so small. I am so used up and deflated.

"Oh, sweetie," Lark says, and I let her put her arms around me, let her pull me toward her and hold me there. "You've done such a good job," she says. "You've done such a good job loving her."

She holds me while I cry, rocks me softly like my mother used to for what now seem like such small hurts—a scraped knee, a playground bully. Now a new pain rips through me at the thought of my mother—not here, not holding me, but in a hospital room, naked like me in a strange place, lost and numb and almost dead.

"I'm going to ask her to stay with me," Lark says softly, letting me go. "Here," she says, looking me in the eye. "Sadie can live here and go to the high school in town for senior year. I've thought about it all summer. But I wanted to ask you first."

"Ask me what?" I say. I don't know what I am supposed to be feeling. Anger? Sadness? Loss? I feel none of those things. What I feel is light-headed. I feel hungry. I want to take a shower.

"What do you think about it?" Lark asks. She grabs my hands in hers and I let her. "What do you think about Sadie staying here?"

"I don't know what I think."

"Max, I know you'd miss her. You're like sisters. I understand that. I know you'd prefer to stay together. But try to think about Sadie for a minute. Try to think about what's best for her."

The rage comes rushing back, stronger than ever. "What do you think I've been doing all these years?" The rage fills me like blood. "I've been thinking about what's best for Sadie my whole fucking life. That's all I've ever thought about. You think you can just decide to be her mother one day and automatically know what to do? Where have you been this whole time? Where were you all these years I've been taking care of her? You're the fucking mother. Where the hell have you been?"

But I am not talking to Lark anymore. I am not talking about Sadie. We hold each other and let our bodies speak apologies. The rage rushes out again, leaving only emptiness, only the place where love should be. We are surrogates for now, holding each other's tears. I can close my eyes and pretend her body is my mother's. I can practice how I really want to hold her, what I really want to say.

Mom, where have you been? Why did you leave us? When are you coming back?

I need you.

I want to go home.

"Close the door," Sadie says, blinking at me through her hangover. "You're letting the light in."

She is huddled into the shadows of the corner of her bed. I am wearing her clothes, standing in front of her, telling her I'm leaving.

"I have to go home," I say. "My mom's sick."

"God, I feel like shit," she says, like she didn't even hear me. She pulls the blankets up to her chin. "What happened last night?"

"You don't remember?"

"Not really," she says. "Something bad happened, didn't it?"

I say nothing. There is nothing to say. She has no idea she kissed me. She has no idea I drowned.

"Wait a minute," she says, as if she just registered what I said, as if the words took that long to travel to her brain. "You can't leave! The summer's not over yet. You can't leave me here alone." She is crying now. She is a child wrapped up in her blanket, as if it could protect her from the world, as if she could be soothed by it's softness always. I sit down on the side of what had been my bed for only a short time.

"Sadie, I have to go. My mom's in the hospital."

She sniffles. Even she knows she can't argue with that. "What happened? Her back again?"

"Yes," I lie. I am not ready to have that conversation with her. I'm not sure I want to, ever. I'm not sure Sadie's the person I want to confide in anymore.

"Oh no, Max. I'm so sorry," she says, and hugs me. This close, I can smell the whiskey still on her breath, the faint scent of vomit. I hold my breath until she lets go.

"I'm leaving tomorrow," I tell her. "I changed my ticket. Doff's giving me a ride to the airport in Omaha first thing in the morning."

"No!" she cries. "That's too soon."

"Sadie, stop being such a drama queen," I say, even though I know I shouldn't. She hates it when I call her that, hates it when anyone discounts her feelings. But I'm so tired, I don't care anymore.

"I'm not a drama queen," she pouts, pulling away deeper into the corner. "I'm sad. Don't you think I have a right to be sad? You're leaving me, Max. You're leaving me here all alone, and you don't even care how I feel about it."

"Sadie," I say. "This isn't about you."

She is quiet. She looks at me like I am some mysterious new thing.

"Is this about last night?" she says carefully. "Is this about something that happened last night?"

When she drinks so much she forgets, Sadie sometimes still feels a tiny echo of the truth—not details of events, but more like their shadows, the aftershocks of their destruction. Her brain may be blank, but her heart and her body hold on to vague memories. They are full of them, full of these indecipherable regrets. I have always been the one to help Sadie make sense of them, to match images to the feelings. But I will not do that this time.

I will let her go. I will give her the freedom to put the pieces together herself.

"Sadie, I think you drink too much," I say.

"What?"

I've never said it, not once, even though I've wanted to all these years. "You scare me, Sadie. It's scary when you get that drunk. You should be able to remember what happened last night."

"Fuck you," she says, her face red with anger.

"What are you going to do when I'm not around anymore? What are you going to do if I'm not there?"

"I don't need you to take care of me." She pushes the blankets off of her. "What makes you think you're so fucking important?"

I say nothing. I don't have an answer for that. I wish I did.

"You're so self-righteous, Max," she says. "You always have been. You've always thought you were so much better than me. Like I couldn't survive without you. Like I'm some useless piece of shit who can't even take care of myself."

"Sadie," I say. "That's not what I meant." But maybe I'm lying. Maybe that is what I meant. Maybe I played a part in her becoming this person who needs me. Maybe I've wanted her to be helpless all this time. Maybe I needed it. Maybe I'm as much to blame as Sadie.

We sit there in silence on the two beds, facing each other but looking in opposite directions. So this is our goodbye. After all these years of friendship. Right now, Sadie thinks it's just for the rest of the summer, but I already know she'll stay here. I'm the only thing she'd have to come back to in Seattle. And we both know that's no longer enough.

"Doff and I are leaving around five tomorrow morning for the airport," I say. "Do you want to come?"

"I don't think so." We're still not looking at each other.

"I'm going to go get my stuff ready," I lie. I have nothing to get ready.

I stand up, wanting out of here, suddenly suffocating.

"You look weird in my clothes," Sadie says, looking up but not at me.

I look down at what I'm wearing—the low-cut tank top, the short shorts that are a little too tight. "I know," I say. "I am nothing like you."

"That's not it," she says. "That's not it at all."

I back out the door, still looking at her, waiting for her to look me in the eye, but she never does. "Bye," I finally say.

"Bye," she says. "See you later." And I don't have the heart or energy to tell her that maybe she won't. At least not for a while. Not for a long time. Maybe not until we are different people and this summer is just a memory. Maybe we will compare notes; maybe we will laugh about how different our stories are. Maybe then I will tell her I forgive her. Maybe then she will have learned that there is so much more to love than that.

I walk back up to the house, grateful for the storm's destruction creating enough new chores to keep me busy until tomorrow morning. I can focus on those instead of the dull ache inside my chest. I almost wish the pain were sharper, more in focus, so I could at least define it, so I could give it a name and make it something ordinary. But this isn't a feeling that fits cleanly into any category. It's messier than that. It's a feeling that will linger. It will morph into different things. It will ebb and flow, rise and fall like tides. It will evaporate with the sun, then fall back down as rain.

I will stop by the barn to say goodbye to the animals. I will say goodbye to Lark. I'll say goodbye to Maria and Joseph and little Bean. I'll probably even say goodbye to Skyler. I'll have the whole car ride to Omaha to say goodbye to Doff, though I'm pretty sure he's not a fan of the mushy stuff, which I'm sure I'll be grateful for. That's all. A handful of people, and a barnful of farm animals.

Nobody's going to throw me a going-away party. I'll slip away at dawn, erasing all traces of myself. People may have a vague feeling that something's missing for a while, but they'll get over it quickly. And all that is fine with me. I don't need to leave a wake, don't need to disrupt people's lives with my comings and goings.

Maybe I won't get the closure I want. But who ever does, anyway? Closure is just some word someone came up with, but I don't think anyone really knows what it is. You leave or are left, and that is the end of the story. It is rarely clean or tidy. Maybe it could last forever if you let it; it could taper off into infinite half-lives, haunting you forever with its slow disintegration.

Or you could decide it's over, leave those loose strings loose, accept that the end is going to be frayed. Maybe that's really what closure is—knowing when it's time to give up on something that's lost its hope. Knowing when it's time to move on to the next thing that shines. Maybe sometimes you have to leave before you're ready to let go; sometimes you have to leave before someone is ready to let go of you. That's the rub of it—if you wait until you're ready to do everything, you'll never get anything done.

ACKNOWLEDGMENTS

Thanks as always to my agent, Amy Tipton, my editor, Anica Mrose Rissi, and everyone at Simon Pulse who helped turn this little story into a book.

Thanks to my high school Latin teacher for naming me Diana. Thanks to Reed College and Hum101 for turning me on to the classics. Thanks to Robert Graves, Plato, Hesiod, and all you crazy people on the Internet who know stuff.

Thanks to John Cameron Mitchell and Stephen Trask for "The Origin of Love" from *Hedwig and the Angry Inch*.

Thanks to the book *Life After Life* by Raymond A. Moody Jr., MD, for teaching me about near-death experiences.

Thanks to Teah and her family for that summer in Iowa so many years ago.

Thanks to Northern California for teaching me all about woo-woo.

Thanks to everyone who grows food.

And a million thanks to Brian—my partner in crime, my best reader, and my forever best friend.

AMY REED is the author of the YA novels *Beautiful*, *Clean*, and *Crazy*. Originally from the Seattle area, she now lives and writes in Oakland, California. Visit her at amyreedfiction.com.